FIREFLY DUET
A Mercy Mountain Novel

Copyright © 2021 by Becca Maxton

All rights reserved. Except for use in any review, the reproduction or utilization of this work in whole or in part in any form by any electronic, mechanical or other means, now known or hereinafter invented, including xerography, photocopying and recording, or in any information storage or retrieval system, is forbidden without the written permission of the publisher.

This is a work of fiction. Names, characters, places and incidents are either the product of the author's imagination or are used fictitiously, and any resemblance to actual persons, living or dead, business establishments, events or locales is entirely coincidental.

Printed in the USA.

Cover Design and Interior Format

A
MERCY MOUNTAIN
NOVEL

Becca Maxton

Dedication

For you. For me.
For all who grieve and rise again.

Chapter 1

New York

"TELL ME ABOUT THE DAY your brother died."

Sofia Russo pressed her forehead against the floor-to-ceiling window of her psychiatrist's seventeenth story office.

"I don't have time." She scanned the Manhattan skyline. "I have to stop at the bank then get to work." She pulled her yellow cashmere wrap tighter. "Your office is freezing, by the way." Her tone softened, deadened. "Anthony was always cold once his cancer progressed."

Dr. Patricia Platt leaned back in her chair. "We could talk about that on Friday."

"Yes." Sofia crossed the room and picked up her bag from the couch. "Okay."

"I'll make sure the office is warmer next visit." Dr. Platt walked her to the door, her hand gently settling on Sofia's shoulder. "We'll work through this together. You didn't do anything wrong, no matter what anyone said. He was sick, Sofia.

There wasn't anything you could do, or not do, that would have prevented his death."

Sofia tapped the side of her head. "I know that here." She tapped her heart. "Not here."

"Yet," Dr. Platt reassured. "You don't know it in your heart, yet. It's only been six weeks. Grief travels its own timeline, and the path is different for everyone."

"Thank you."

In the elevator, Sofia placed her bag on the floor and, leaning down, dug through its contents to pull her wallet from beneath her camera equipment. The bank was close, just a short distance across the small courtyard ahead. After the bank, she'd have to take a cab to her photo shoot at the theater to make it on time.

Outside, the hot, humid August air felt good after the chilly office. She hurried along, her new sling-back pumps forming blisters on blisters with every step. In the vestibule of the bank lobby, she stopped at the ATM and inserted her debit card. With shaking hands, she put Anthony's last paycheck as football coach at Port Vincent High School in the deposit envelope and fed it into the machine.

In a couple weeks, Anthony's players would start a new season. Autumn had once been her favorite — windy days, leaves blowing off the trees, and the scent of apple cider. The best part of the fall was sitting in the stands with her parents and her brother's girlfriend for Friday night games.

She shook her head, forcing her thoughts

back to the present. Pressing another button, she extracted the receipt from the machine and stuffed it in her wallet. The door to the bank crashed open, slamming into her side and almost tossing her on her ass.

"Ouch! Take it easy." Looking up she met dark brown eyes, the only visible features surrounded by a ski mask.

The man shook his head, as if to say she were a naughty little girl. "Back up. Get on the floor."

As she retreated, her hip struck the side of the ATM and she winced, crouching next to it. Two men dressed in black trench coats and carrying bags walked through the door held by the gunman. Not a sound interrupted the men's precise movements as they passed through the vestibule to the outside.

Balancing a few feet from the gunman, Sofia teetered on her uncomfortable heels. When she shifted, her bag tilted dislodging the contents. Her camera landed with a noisy thud, sending a lens cap skittering across the floor. The gunman's gaze met hers for a split second before he turned, firing two rapid shots through the door leading inside the bank.

Flinching, she fell forward on her knees. Her hands slammed onto the floor, catching her before she landed face first. Her left wrist buckled and nearly gave out, sending pinpricks radiating up her arm.

A whiz and another loud pop jerked her attention back to the gunman, who dropped to his knees and crumpled onto his side. His fall blocked the door, leaving it open to the inside of the bank.

Her ears rang with sudden sound – screaming, squealing tires, and sirens. She moved inside the bank, her focus on the security guard's uniformed body lying still on the floor. A thin strip of black fabric ran along the side of his pantleg. Crimson began coloring outside the line, turning the dark material a rusty purple.

"Help me!" She motioned to a woman rushing forward from inside the bank. Sofia unbuckled the strap from her bag, slipped it under the guard's leg, and fastened it tight above the wound as a tourniquet. Her left arm throbbed and burned. Grimacing through the pain, she pulled her lightweight wrap from her purse and placed it over the guard's gunshot wound. Gasping, she folded her injured arm against her chest and with her right hand, pressed hard against the wound to stanch the bleeding.

Don't die. Don't die. Don't die on me!

A small sob of relief escaped her when the guard opened his eyes. Panicked, he tried to sit up, grabbing onto her injured arm. She scooted out of his reach as knife-like pain shot through her wrist. He shook his head from side to side, his eyes wide.

"Don't be afraid," she said as calmly as she could. "Lie back. You're going to be okay." She resumed her prior position, pressing her right forearm over the gaping hole in his thigh as she listened to his labored breathing.

A blur of blue drove past her, heading into the chaos inside the bank. A low rough voice penetrated. "You're doing good. Keep the pressure on. They'll be here soon."

After what seemed an eternity, metal grated on metal as gurney legs were raised, announcing the arrival of the emergency staff. They hauled the ancient piece of equipment across the lobby, rickety wheels wobbling like a defective grocery cart. She continued holding pressure on the wound.

"We'll take over," said an authoritative yet gentle voice as Sofia was lifted beneath her arms and set aside. "Your wrist looks broken. You'll ride in the ambulance," the EMT ordered as he bandaged the guard's leg while his partner administered a shot and inserted an IV.

"Let's move." The emergency staff strapped the guard's lower legs and upper chest with safety belts and lifted him onto the gurney.

"My bag." Sofia pointed. One of the bank employees tucked her bag under her good arm. Outside, an enormous crowd of spectators and police officers had gathered. Cameras clicked and people shouted as she walked behind the gurney.

With the customary two bangs on the door, the ambulance was off, moving in fast spurts with sirens on and lights flaring. Blood dried on her hands and forearms, tightening against her skin. The material of her dress was blotted with red fingerprints, her lap soaked. They wove through traffic, slowing, then accelerating at each intersection before arriving at the hospital, where the guard was whisked away. She emerged from the ambulance and nodded when the police officer told her he'd be back in a moment.

"You can sit here, miss," a nurse told her, leading her to an examination area across from the nurses' station and wrapping a blanket around her shoulders. "Someone will take a look at your arm."

"Yes." A wave of nausea hit as she stared at the golf-ball-size bump forming near the base of her hand. According to the big clock on the wall, it was eight-forty. Her eyes followed the clock's red second hand as it made a complete rotation. A perfect circle of blood stared back at her from one of her pretty new shoes.

"Will he live?" Sofia blurted.

The nurse glanced her direction. "They're doing everything they can for him."

"They'll keep him warm too? Because he can't be cold." Sofia glanced at the empty hallway.

The automatic doors to the hospital emergency entrance slid open and Dr. Platt ran toward her. "Sofia? Oh my God, are you okay? I saw police cars out my office window right after you left. There are pictures of you on the news. I got here as fast as I could. I called your parents. Thank God you're all right."

"You have to help him. He's cold. Please."

"Who's cold, Sofia?"

"Anthony. He's cold. I let him get cold." Pulled into Dr. Platt's arms, Sofia collapsed, sobbing against her. "Please."

"It's okay, Sofia. It's not Anthony. It's not Anthony."

"For Christ's sake," Jim Mannis said to the captain as he ran his hand along the back of his neck, realizing he'd better ask his sister, Kai, for a haircut when he got home. The captain's rubber-soled shoes audibly gripped the marble floor of the police station. Jim kept stride as the captain spoke.

"It was a bank robbery with a shooting. You shot the shooter. We have to put you on official leave while we investigate. It's standard procedure. Tell me what happened first."

Jim stopped walking and closed his eyes. "I wasn't on duty until noon today. We were on our way to get coffee."

"You and Rafe?" The captain asked.

"Right. Rafe needed some cash before his flight, so we stop across the street from the bank. I see a military vehicle."

"And?"

Gripping the back of his neck, Jim sighed. "It's not really a military vehicle. It's just a fucking Hummer parked in front of a fucking bank. But my heart starts racing as if Rafe and I are back in Afghanistan. That's when we see two guys exiting the bank and another holding the door with his gun aimed at someone."

"Sofia Russo," the captain said.

"I don't know who the hell it is. Rafe starts adjusting his ball cap low on his head. It's a nervous habit he got from the Army. He used to do the same thing with his helmet. The next second he starts calling it out just like he's my spotter again."

The captain motioned for them to keep walking. "Go on."

Jim replayed the scene in his head, his voice taking on a clipped reporting style. "Woman in a white dress. Movement at the door. Shots fired. I'm on instinct. I stand, aim, fire my weapon. Gunman drops."

He followed the captain into his office and closed the door. Lined with shelves filled with every type of Yankees' paraphernalia imaginable, the captain's office resembled an eleven-year-old boy's bedroom.

"I gave notice two weeks ago. It's only a few days early," Jim continued. "If I leave now, I can be on an airplane home to Colorado this afternoon. You've done a lot for me, Captain."

"Are you sure you still want to leave New York? You've built a solid reputation here in just three years. It's impressive."

"Thank you, sir. I'm sure. My dad, he's getting up there." Jim tapped his fingers on the edge of the desk, unsure about saying more. "He asked me a few months ago to consider coming home this year. I said no to him once before when he wanted help and stayed away eighteen years just to make sure he got the point." He straightened his shoulders as the captain nodded.

"Making up for lost time. I understand. And I am sorry you can't go immediately. You'll need to remain available and here a little longer. You'll get paid."

He didn't care about pay. With his decision made to leave, he just wanted to shower and go home. Home meaning home, and not one more day in New York City.

"There's another thing—you've been requested down at the courthouse tomorrow to meet the witness. Her family will be there. They know you're coming."

"What for?"

The captain cleared his throat. "Sofia Russo. She's the woman in the white dress all over the Internet. She wouldn't leave the hospital last night until we promised she'd get a meeting to thank the man who saved her life. That's you. Funny thing, she's the one who saved the bank guard. The media is all over her story. Here. Take a look at these."

The captain moved around his desk, settling closer to Jim as he swiped through photos on his phone. "These are pictures taken at the scene by news photographers and bystanders. You were there. She singlehandedly put a tourniquet on the guard's leg, stanched the wound, and that's a picture of her holding the guard's hand before the EMTs took him to the ambulance."

Jim studied the first photo. Yeah, he'd been there all right, but more like a world away. He'd caught a glimpse of her. Another photo showed her gazing at the injured man. *Is she smiling?* He took the phone out of the captain's hand and held it closer for a second and then farther away. Jesus, he needed his eyes checked. *Rafe is right—all the parts start failing after thirty-five.* "What's with her weird smile?"

The captain shrugged. "In the last twenty-four

hours, she's established quite a reputation for herself as a sexy Florence Nightingale. I told you, the media can't get enough of her."

"Who's Florence Nightingale?"

"A famous nurse in history. Sofia's sweet, you know?"

Jim raised his eyebrows.

"What?" the captain said with an embarrassed glance. "She spent the night in the hospital comforting the guard's mother. Oh, and the kid you shot —is still in a coma. We can't speak to him."

Jim put his hands on his hips and hung his head. "Kid?"

"Nineteen, so technically, not a kid. In any case, son, you saved that woman's life. You're a fine officer. We wouldn't have hired you otherwise. Or brought in your buddy Rafe to help with training our guys." He clapped his hand on Jim's shoulder. "She was lucky you happened to be there. More important, we don't want the lovely Miss Russo to miss her chance to meet her hero."

Why is there never a window or an escape hatch when I need one?

"Listen, this is the third robbery in the last six weeks," the captain continued. "The FBI is on it. Assistant D.A. Nader wants this meeting bad. Take attention off the city looking like dipshits because we haven't caught these guys."

"Have Rafe meet her."

The captain walked back around his desk and sat down. "He's already on a plane."

His buddy knew when to make an exit. He was loyal, not stupid.

"Rafe wasn't the one with the gun. Besides, he's not NYPD like you. He's just a contractor. Another great contribution you made when you suggested him, by the way. Anyway, a few more days, that's all I'm asking for."

Fantastic.

Jim examined the photo of Sofia Russo again. She was a mess—but pretty. He hadn't been on a date in a year. Make that laid. He hadn't been laid in a year. He adjusted his stance. His sex life, or lack thereof, was irrelevant to this situation. "Hell." Jim shook his head.

"Quite a looker, isn't she?" The captain grinned when Jim handed his phone back. "By the way, Lieutenant Kincaid will be at the courthouse tomorrow too."

"Why's that?"

"He knows the family. I guess his daughter is Sofia Russo's best friend."

Chapter 2

LATE AFTERNOON THE NEXT DAY, Jim opened the door to a small windowless conference room at the courthouse. The meeting with the Russo family was already in full swing. Except for a nod from Lieutenant Kincaid, he entered the room unnoticed. All the chairs were occupied, so he leaned against the back wall and surveyed the group.

It didn't take more than a five-minute search on his laptop last night to find photos of the whole family, including a son, Anthony, who died recently. Mr. and Mrs. Russo and Sofia sat at one side of the table, Assistant District Attorney Sharon Nader and Lieutenant Jack Kincaid on the other side.

"No, thank you," Sofia Russo said as she sat back in her seat.

Sharon Nader adjusted the buttons of her boring brown suit jacket straining against rolls of barely contained heft. "Miss Russo, you have been through a traumatic event, no doubt, so surely you can understand why it may be best to consider some precautions."

When she stood, Jim sized Sofia up – or rather, down. She was a tiny thing, shorter than the pictures revealed. She might be all of five feet two and very pretty. Her deep brown hair settled in loose curls around the sides of ample breasts. He allowed his eyes to linger there longer than he should. No matter, her attention was focused solely on the D.A.

"I see no reason to believe I'm in any sort of danger. I can't identify the other suspects. They wore masks."

If this were a cheesy cop movie, Sharon Nader would win an Oscar. She stood, putting her hands forward on the table, and leaned in. "We need to work toward some kind of understanding here. This is about a robbery, and yes, there is still danger."

Jim's limited experience with Nader showed she damn sure didn't react well if she felt challenged, which was often. Including now with Sofia Russo, who appeared up for a fight.

"I think what the D.A. is concerned about is the media harassment –" Lieutenant Kincaid began only to be interrupted when Sofia put her hand on the table too.

"There is one reason I came here today and that's to say thank you to the person who saved my life. That was our agreement. Then I'm going back to *my* life."

Jim bowed his head, stifling a smile.

"Frank, do something," said Mrs. Russo.

Nader sighed and sat again in her chair, which creaked in protest.

"Everyone needs to calm down," Frank Russo said. "Jack, I'm not sure your idea is a good one. We just lost Anthony six weeks ago. Sofia could have been killed in front of that bank. Having her leave right now doesn't seem right, even if there are –"

"There are what?" Sofia asked. "What idea? Who said anything about me leaving New York?"

Jim shifted his stance, biting back an oath. *Shit. There must be threats. Any high publicity event brings out the crazies.*

"Perhaps Officer Mannis could join in and explain the details for Miss Russo." Nader's sarcastic suggestion brought everyone's attention in his direction.

For the first time, Sofia Russo's big brown eyes met his. "So you're in on this too?" she said acknowledging his presence. "Whatever *this* is."

"Actually, I haven't had a chance to brief Officer Mannis yet," Lieutenant Kincaid said.

Jim pushed off the wall to stand at full height; her gaze followed him up. Stepping forward he offered his hand. "Hi, Sofia. We haven't been introduced. I'm Jim Mannis. I was at the scene yesterday."

"Officer Mannis is the one who shot the gunman," Lieutenant Kincaid said.

His heart gave a funny skip when tears welled in her eyes. "Like you, I'm not exactly sure what's going on here at the moment. But there must be a legitimate concern if your parents, the D.A., and

Lieutenant Kincaid want to discuss your safety." He leaned closer. "Even if it feels a little like an ambush."

"It was you?"

He stepped back, gaining distance only to find himself suddenly engulfed in her mother's embrace.

"We can never thank you enough. You saved our daughter."

"Thank you, Officer Mannis." Frank Russo stood and shook his hand. "We're very grateful to you. If Sofia has to leave, we can't think of anyone else she'd be safer with than you."

What the hell? "Sir?"

Despite all the blood draining from his head, Jim kept his tone respectful. "Lieutenant, should we step outside and…"

He stopped speaking when Sofia grabbed his arm.

"Oh no." She shook her head. "You're not going anywhere, and neither is anyone else." She held onto him as if she could keep a man his size from leaving the room if she tried.

"Really, Dad?" she continued. "This is your plan? And, Mr. Kincaid, you've known me practically my whole life. Do you think I'm going to sit here doing nothing while you manhandle me right out of New York?"

After a squeeze, she let go of his bicep and walked around the table. Her wrist cast landed on the table with a tiny thud. "What is going on that I don't know?"

Damn. Way to command the room.

Going for an appearance of calm, Jim leaned against the wall as the others took their seats again. He'd already decided to quit the force and go home to take care of his dad and renovate the family lodge. He didn't want to be signed up for babysitting a stranger, even if she was beautiful.

"I agree. Let's get everything in the open and then hammer out details," Nader said. "We need to defuse media attention as quickly as possible. Sofia, there are threats against your life and that's why a plan for you to leave New York was discussed earlier."

"Death threats? Against me? But, why? What did I do?"

"It happens. All sorts of nuts, and normal people too, for that matter, have seen the videos of you at the robbery scene all covered in blood. They know you tied a tourniquet on the guard, and he's going to make a full recovery. But there's a particular part of one of the videos posted online that is sparking controversy. We believe the intense attention on this has led to the threats."

It impressed him that her first question was to ask if her parents or the bank guard were in any danger.

"We don't believe so," Lieutenant Kincaid said, carrying the story forward. "But to be safe we have an officer at the hospital and surveillance on your folks' house. The good news is there have been no specific threats directed toward any of them."

"I want to see the video." Sofia emphasized the request with a determined nod. "You said there is something about it. I should watch it."

"That's not a good idea," Frank Russo responded. "It's…people are interpreting things incorrectly, honey…there's been a misunderstanding."

Mrs. Russo let out a puff of air. "Frank, you're doing it again. Someone tell Sofia the whole story so she can understand *why* this is so important. And for God's sake, Officer Mannis needs to be brought up to speed too."

Jim pushed off the wall when Nader got up and offered her seat to him before she spoke.

"About thirty minutes ago, we assigned two officers to your apartment building."

"Why?"

"Your window facing the street was smashed with a brick that had a note attached that said, 'We'll get you, bitch.' We've secured the area and you'll be safe. I don't know if you are aware, Sofia, that the gunman lived through the night. He died two hours ago. His name is Lewis Nabb. He was nineteen years old and a popular athlete at a local university. We've learned his older brother belonged to a gang involved in a string of robberies. We believe, unfortunately, that's why he participated. The part of the video everyone is cryptically referring to is when you crawled by Nabb's body on your way to help the bank guard.

"I crawled?" Sofia stared at the assistant D.A. "I don't remember."

"The controversy is about you seeming to choose one man's life over another. This has sparked a backlash on social media and the public is eating it up."

"You're saying I crawled by a dying man? People think I let him die?"

"Yes." Nader took a deep breath in through her nose, out through her mouth, as if she practiced this move regularly. "Officer Mannis, we're proposing you leave soon, tomorrow in fact, and that you take Miss Russo with you. Temporarily. It's not necessary at a formal witness protection level. But these threats are no joke. There's no need to take chances."

"Oh, honey," Mrs. Russo said when Sofia put her head on the table, her shoulders shaking.

"I had to stop the bleeding. I don't remember crawling. I don't remember everything."

"You reacted in the moment." Her mother rested her hand on the middle of Sofia's back. "What you did was save a man's life. There is absolutely nothing for you to feel bad about."

"I wouldn't suggest time away if I didn't think it was the best option," Lieutenant Kincaid said. "Jim, I apologize for springing this on you. I wasn't able to reach you before the meeting and everything escalated when Nabb died. Sofia, I've known Jim for three years and your family since you and my daughter were nine years old. You're just as much a daughter to me as Delia. If this were happening to her, I'd want her to go."

How many military missions had Jim been on where orders came less than twenty-four hours before departure? This situation was unorthodox maybe, but not new territory.

"I understand the situation, sir," he said.

"It's settled then," Frank Russo responded.

Sofia lifted her head, brushing the back of her hand to a tear-stained cheek. "I haven't agreed to this, Dad."

"She's right, this is ultimately her decision." Jim got up and walked to the door then turned back. "If I can help, I'm willing. How about I step out for a moment."

"Wait."

He maintained steady eye contact as Sofia studied his face. When she rewarded him with a tiny smile, he responded with a brusque nod.

"Could everyone excuse us, please. I'd like to speak to Officer Mannis for a moment." She tilted her chin, gesturing toward the door. "Alone."

He avoided any appearance of surprise at the request, instead holding the door open while her parents and the lieutenant left the room. Downright testy, Sharon Nader gave a huff and marched by him into the hallway. "I have another meeting. Give me a report when you're done, Mannis."

"Will do." He quietly closed the conference room door.

"She's pissed, huh?"

Jim nodded. "I'll deny I told you this, but some people refer to her as Vader. Not me." He added, his hand over his heart. "She can be prickly, but she's a good D.A."

"I want to see the video."

"Are you sure?"

She tilted her head, her expression scolding. "I'm sure."

"Okay." He sat down next to her and scrolled

through his phone to bring up news stories of the robbery. When he found the part after he'd shot the gunman, he held the phone between them and pressed play.

"Oh my God. I did. I crawled right past him as if he wasn't even there. Oh my God."

Jim turned off his phone and set it on the table. She sat with her eyes closed, her hand on her forehead. He didn't try to fill the silence until after several minutes passed. "A couple things your mother mentioned earlier are right on the mark."

She opened her eyes. "Like what?"

"First, you were reacting under extraordinary circumstances. In a survival situation, some people run. Some people freeze. You didn't hesitate to help and as a result, your actions saved a man's life. Second, your mom told you there is nothing to be ashamed of, and she's correct. There isn't."

Her watery eyes pleaded with his. "I still chose. I chose who I helped, didn't I?"

"No." He shook his head. "Your mind focused your attention on the guard. The person who wasn't a threat."

She sniffled, her laugh soft. "You speak as if my brain has a mind of its own."

He took advantage of the small lift in mood and smiled. "It's sort of like that. Our hereditary brain—sometimes people call it our reptilian brain—is all instinct and not about conscious thought. When you're in a pressure situation, like a violent crime or war, survival takes over. Also, the reality is not everyone makes it."

"You made a choice though. I'm alive because of it."

He glanced her way. "That's my job and my training."

"Is that why you're agreeing with this plan for me to go with you?"

"You could say that. Plus, I have a lot of respect for Lieutenant Kincaid. I already made

the decision to leave New York and gave my notice before the robbery. I have family obligations." He paused. It wasn't necessary to go into detail. "What do you think? It's four-thirty and if we're leaving tomorrow, there's a lot to do." He pushed his chair from the table, stood, and put his phone in his back pocket.

"I guess it seems a good idea to let things settle down. Okay, we can tell everyone I'll go."

"Good. I'll put things in motion." He offered his hand to help her stand. She shifted from one foot to the other as he towered over her. "Is there something else?"

"I feel like we should hug…or something."

He chuckled, caught off guard. "You do?"

"Is that okay? You saved my life."

Tough one minute, tender the next. The contradiction drew him in like a magnet and he opened his arms. "I'll take a hug."

Nodding, she stepped forward and he wrapped her in his embrace. She rested against him, her head on his chest, and he felt an all over sigh leave her body. He shifted, adjusting his stance when she leaned back, looking up.

"Thank you."

Chapter 3

"I'LL ARRANGE A RIDE FOR tomorrow night and pick you up at your apartment," Jim said. "We'll take a red-eye to Denver."

Her former self, before Anthony's death, would have spent the day shopping and packing for a trip. But this was no ordinary occasion like a vacation to the beach or going on a cruise. She wasn't sure what she was in for. Or for how long. As if she'd been granted a wish from above, her mother offered to ship more clothing and items after Sofia arrived and knew what she'd need most.

The next morning, escorted by a police officer, Sofia arrived at the offices for *Stage* magazine intent on finishing one last project at work. She arranged photos of the cast in the typical format of the theater's program book for an upcoming play staring her best friend, Delia Kincaid. The PR staff had avoided giving her any grief for how late the marketing materials were. She ignored her phone vibrating as long as possible, then eventually scrolled through texts from her boss, Robert, and headed upstairs to his office.

In the stairwell, her phone vibrated again, then rang a moment later and she answered. To say Robert seemed unhappy as he fired off questions proved an understatement. She stopped mid-way up the steps.

Did she know he'd been trying to reach her?

Did she understand the program book was too late?

Did she realize this forced him to hire someone else to finish it?

She gripped the railing listening to Robert sigh before he continued. "The fact is, your work has been suffering, since…well…"

Since my brother's death, he means. His statement rang true. "I can do better." She squeezed back tears, listening to the desperation in her own voice. An absence now would not go over well. "I'm on my way up to your office. I have to leave New York for a short time, so I wanted to speak with you about that."

"Sofia," Robert said, his voice taking on a dangerously gentle tone, "I like you. You know that."

But.

"This is a difficult time for you. I've tried to be comforting, even outside of work. Truth is, we didn't exactly light the world on fire, did we?"

Unbelievable.

In the middle of lecturing her, he critiqued their one and only night together. She cringed, shaking off the memory as if a spider crawled up her neck. A poor decision made out of loneliness.

He's probably been searching for an excuse to get rid

of me.

"This job is important to me. I need to keep some sort of stability. This is short notice, I know. It would only be a couple weeks. It's related to the robbery…and social media…there are threats against me and people are upset —"

"It's business, Sofia."

She leaned her head against the wall when he interrupted her rambling.

"Look at it this way. Maybe this is a good thing. You can relax and heal that broken wrist. Here's what I'll do. I'm going to pay you for the current project. Technically, we don't owe you the entire amount since you didn't finish the work, but there's no need to part on bad terms. As soon as we hang up, I'll ask Nancy to prepare a check for you. You can pick it up on your way out."

"Robert, please."

"Call me when you get back in town. Maybe we can work something out then."

The phone went dead as she slumped down on a step. Tapping her cast on her forehead, she imagined the game she and Anthony used to play when they were little. Grabbing his arm, she'd use his hand to playfully slap the top of his head and tease, "Why are you hitting yourself?" The memory of his little boy giggles ghosted through her ears.

"Have Nancy mail the check instead," she one-finger texted to Robert. *Asshole.* Marching down the steps, she slammed her good hand on the red release lever to the emergency door, smiling when it set off the building alarm.

"You tell me what you want out of here," Delia called from inside the closet, "and I'll pack it for you."

Sofia stepped around the corner and shrugged at her best friend. Moving to the bed, she knelt and pulled a suitcase from underneath.

"Sof, come on." Delia leaned a shoulder on the closet doorframe. "You have one bag half-packed and it's less than two hours before the car is coming to take you to the airport. So far, you're bringing makeup and a hair dryer. You do realize they have drugstores where you're going."

"You're right. I need to get my camera equipment together."

"You need to bring some clothes." Delia moved to the bed, sat, and patted the mattress beside her. "Sit for a second. Talk to me."

Sofia sunk down on the bed. "I got fired."

"What! That dick, Robert. You're the best photographer the theater has ever had." Delia put an arm around her shoulders. "You know, the latest program book was done by some schmuck he hired. Let me tell you. It sucks. Seriously. The whole cast is angry because we look like crap." Delia jumped up and struck a pose – her hip jutting out, her face scrunched like a crabby cat. "In one of the photos I appear completely constipated."

Sofia snort-laughed and fell back on the bed.

"I'm not exaggerating. If they use that photo for the giant banner in front of the theater, I will bust Robert's nuts. God, I cannot believe he fired you. I'm so sorry."

"Jim Mannis has no idea the mess he's dragging with him to Colorado. Poor guy." Sofia stared at the ceiling.

"There's no poor guy about it. You are *not* a mess. Believe me, he's probably just like my father, and loves this. Savior complex and all." Delia grabbed her phone from her purse. "We don't have much time. Let's finish packing so we can give you a proper margarita send off."

Twenty-five minutes later, Sofia's two suitcases, camera bag, and purse were stacked by the door. She followed the sound of the blender to the kitchen.

"All packed," Sofia said.

Picking up two glasses and the pitcher of margaritas, Delia came around the counter and nudged her. "Let's sit on the floor by your half boarded up window and look at the city until your ride shows up."

The view from Sofia's apartment was ordinary and nothing compared to her friend's high-rise Manhattan spread. For all Delia's attention-seeking on Broadway, she kept surprisingly discreet about her fame. She saved all her energy for the audience. And for being the best friend a woman could ask for since the fourth grade.

Flopping down on the cream-colored carpet, Sofia leaned her back against the couch. "What am I going to do without you for the next few weeks?"

"Tell me about Officer Mannis." Delia smiled

over the rim of her glass. "What's he like?"

She contemplated how to best describe Jim. *Handsome? Tall?* "He's formidable," she began tentatively. "Maybe six-four and muscles." She flexed her good arm. "He's confident," she added gaining some momentum, "and he kind of has this grin, as if he knows what's going to happen before anyone else does." She paused, taking several gulps of a drink that tasted like straight tequila.

"Oh, really now? Tell me the part you're not telling me."

"What do you mean?"

"Your neck is all blotchy and red. I know what that means. Spill it. I take it he's good-looking."

Sofia ran her fingers through the carpet, pulling it up in tufts. "I guess you could say that."

"I am *so* checking this guy out when he gets here." Delia keeled over dramatically on her side and slapped the floor.

"Don't say anything embarrassing."

"No worries. I'm just going to make sure he's properly prepared to take care of my girl."

An hour and more margaritas later, the intercom buzzed. Delia beat her to the door and pressed the button. "Hello, this is Florence Nightingale, how may I help you?"

"It's Jim Mannis. Sofia? Is that you?"

Sofia swatted at Delia's arm and gently shoved her aside. "Hi, I'll be down in just a minute."

"I'll come up and help carry your luggage."

Delia put the back of her hand to her forehead. "Why, I do declare, Officer, that would be right kindly of you."

"Shhhh!" Sofia laughed, forgetting to let go of the button.

"What was that?" Jim asked.

"Nothing. Thank you." She pressed the button long enough to give him time to enter the building and then pointed at Delia with a smirk. "You, babe, are a little bit drunk."

"Oh, and you aren't?"

"I stopped after one drink. Why don't you go find your purse and shoes? I can get you a cab home."

"Right." Delia licked her lips and headed down the hall toward the bedroom.

A minute later, Sofia opened the door at Jim's knock. "Come in." She stepped aside so he could enter.

"The driver got to my place a little early, so if you need a few more minutes…" His glance slid past her toward the hallway.

"This must be Officer Mannis." Delia used the wall for balance as she hopped, trying to put her shoe on. Finally successful, she sauntered over and offered a hand. "Hi, I'm Delia."

"It's nice to meet you," Jim answered.

"It's nice to meet *you*. I'm very glad you are taking care of the girl. Our girl. My girl."

Sofia cleared her throat, shaking Delia out of staring with a goofy grin.

"I'm Jack Kincaid's daughter."

"I think very highly of your father. He's a good man." Jim walked back toward the door, turning as Delia shimmied her shoulders and mouthed *he's hot!* Sofia glanced at Jim and pressed her lips together.

"Okay, then. I'll just take your suitcases to the car and let you ladies say goodbye."

Sofia put her head back, watching out the window as the driver headed to LaGuardia. The light from Jim's phone lit up the backseat and eventually roused her curiosity. "Is everything okay with our flight?"

He didn't look up. "Yep. Just checking the weather at the other end. No wind. We should have a smooth trip."

"How long is the flight?

"A little over four hours. From there, we'll rent a car. It's another hour and half drive to Ashnee Valley. We should get to my dad's place," he rocked his head to the side, "around seven in the morning. That doesn't take into account the time change. It's going to be a long night. Sorry."

"That's okay. I appreciate everything you're doing. I just hope I'm not too big a burden on you or your family."

His eyes settled directly on hers. "Let's make a deal. There is no burden, okay?"

"Delia says men like her dad, and you, enjoy this sort of thing because of a savior complex." Sofia grinned.

His hoot of laughter drew a glance in the rearview mirror from the driver. "I'm military and a cop, honey. Of course, I have a savior complex."

His endearment, *honey,* didn't mean anything.

Still, the fact that it made her pulse speed up preoccupied her – during their arrival at the airport, through the baggage and security check, and when boarding the plane.

"We're in row four A and B. Are you okay with the window?" Jim asked. "The aisle gives me a little more leg room."

"We're flying first class?" Her voice lifted in surprise as she slid over and shoved her camera bag and purse under the seat in front of her.

"You bet. This trip is on Nader's dime."

After takeoff and the plane's reaching thirty-thousand feet according to the pilot's announcement, she felt suspended in time. Caught mid-air between her past and an unknown future, only the present moment remained. She glanced at Jim's profile. With his eyes closed, she could study his five o'clock shadow and full lips. He had the perfect nose for a man, not too big, not crooked. Great eyebrows. Sofia jerked her head back, when he opened one eye peeking at her. Pulling her purse from under the seat, she dug through it, hoping it took attention from the fact she was checking him out. "Were you sleeping?"

He shifted, sitting up as the flight attendant headed down the aisle, handing out bags of peanuts. "Not really."

"Good. Because maybe we should talk and get to know each other." She swore he groaned, then tried to play if off by stretching his arms out in front of him.

"Sure. How about twenty questions?"

She scrunched her nose. "Like the game, where

you guess what the other person is thinking?"

"Oh, right. Okay, no, not exactly the game. Instead, we each ask the other person twenty questions." Opening the small bag of peanuts the flight attendant gave him, he leaned his head back and poured the contents in his mouth.

She considered his idea and opened her bag of nuts. "What if there's a question one of us doesn't want to answer?"

"What do you mean, like, can you take a pass?"

"Exactly. Say I ask you a question…" she waved her hand in the air "…and you're too timid to answer." She stared straight ahead and popped another peanut in her mouth, snickering with a glance his direction when he coughed.

"You're worried about me being shy?" His eyes widened as he spoke. "Okay, we each get one pass if there's a question with a topic that's off limits. I'll start. What's your favorite color?"

She laughed. "Yellow. Okay, my turn. What's yours?"

"Pass," he said with a grin. "It's blue."

"Very cute. Your turn again."

The game progressed through a series of tame questions in which she learned his favorite sport, football. Animal he thought sexiest, cheetah. Age, thirty-six, seven years older than she. Best book, *Of Mice and Men*. And somehow not-so-surprising favorite band, Van Halen.

"How old were you when you had your first kiss?"

"Eleven." Sofia answered. "You?"

"Seven."

"No way. Do you have any tattoos?"

"Yes, this is one of them." He pushed his sleeve up revealing a tree-of-life. "So, have you ever been in love?"

She pulled her chin back. "Wow, that's a serious question. No. How about you?"

He shook his head. "Love, no. Lust, yes."

"Mmm, I hear you." Her cheeks warmed. "Number of siblings?"

"Two. I have a sister named Kai."

"And…?" She asked when he didn't continue.

He took a swallow of his drink and set it back on the tray in front of him. "Pass."

"For real? As in, you aren't going to say if you *have* another brother or sister?"

"Brother."

She didn't press for more detail. "So if you could live your life again, knowing what you do now, what would you change?" She set her hand on his arm. "Oops, it's your turn. You go."

"Okay, would you rather be married with kids or have ten million dollars?"

She chewed her bottom lip, her eyes meeting his for a second. "I guess I should make sure my parents have at least one grandchild … I'm their only chance now." She lifted her hand from his arm. "Pass."

"Stupid question. Sorry."

She offered a quick smile. "No, it wasn't. It's all right."

"I want go back to your question, about what I'd change if I could do things over."

"All right."

"I'd have had the courage to stay near my family after my mother died. I wouldn't have left... for so long. It sure as hell would make going back easier now."

Chapter 4

Colorado

THE SKY TURNED FROM DARK to soft pink to brilliant blue as Jim drove them toward Ashnee Valley.

"Let's stop for coffee," he said. "We can have breakfast when we reach the house. We gained a couple hours back with the time difference. My dad is up early most days, but not this early and I'd rather not wake him."

"Coffee sounds good. So, that's who we're staying with, your dad?"

"I'm planning for you to stay with him. He has a spare bedroom and he'd enjoy the company. My sister's house is full of kids, so that's out. And I'll be occupied a lot of the time. Plus, in a couple more weeks Rafe will be living with me too."

"Who's Rafe?"

"Army buddy. Actually, he's more than that. I met him when I was still in high school. He's about fourteen years older than me, something like that. He lived in Ashnee Valley for a summer doing some work for Dad. Things were a little rough then." Jim shrugged. "He helped me get my shit together. Find direction. Join the Army. Anyway, it would be pretty boring hanging out alone at my house."

"Oh."

He glanced at her. "Is that okay?"

"Of course. That sounds perfect. I really appreciate everything…" Darn her voice that wavered and faded out as she turned to look out the window.

"I'll be around," he continued. "The house I'm moving into is only about fifteen minutes from Dad's. It could be fun for you. He has chickens, a couple pigs, and an ancient horse. Besides all the cattle. Have you ever been around animals?"

"Not unless pigeons count."

He chuckled. "You'll see some cool birds like hawks, falcons, and eagles. You said you're a photographer. I bet you can take pictures of all sorts of wildlife while you're here." She perked up a little at his suggestion, offering him a small smile.

After they made a short stop and were on the road another hour, Jim made a turn and drove under the wooden arch to the Mannis ranch. Sofia studied the small home straight ahead, the barns to the left, and the pasture dotted with cows to the right. She gave Jim a curious look when he parked next to a vehicle that appeared a cross between an old milk truck and a very small ambulance.

"That mess belongs to Leo, my sister, Kai's, husband. He's a nurse. He and my sister both work at a clinic in town and believe it or not, he makes house calls. Mostly, he likes the fact there is a freezer in it where he keeps ice cream bars to give to kids." Jim shut off the engine, then came around to open her door. "He's eccentric."

"He sounds nice." Sofia stepped out of the car and took a deep breath.

"Don't worry, everybody is looking forward to meeting you." With his hand on the small of her back, he directed her up five steps to a side entrance into the house.

The kitchen asserted itself as cheery, with a bright yellow-and-red-flowered tablecloth on a small kitchen table. Matching half-curtains hung over the windows. An old-style refrigerator was deep crimson. Plenty of people in New York would pay a fortune for something as unique as a red vintage appliance.

Turning from the sink, a woman Sofia guessed must be Jim's sister wiped her hands on a dishtowel. She grinned, made her way to Jim, and gave him a hug. "I'm so glad you're home. Dad. Leo. They're here," she called. "And you must be Sofia. You're so pretty. Aw, look at your wrist. Can I give you a hug?" Kai didn't wait for an answer before pulling her in.

"Kai, calm down." Jim shook his head and smiled as the swinging door to the kitchen opened. He introduced her next to Leo, who had to be six-seven at least. He made Jim look small by comparison. An image of Leo squeezing himself into the strange little truck outside almost made Sofia laugh out loud. She focused her attention on Jim's father for his introduction.

"Sofia, this is my father, Ben Mannis. Dad, this is Sofia Russo."

"It's a pleasure to meet you, Mr. Mannis."

"You can call me Ben," Jim's father said. "After all, we're going to be living together. Do you cook?" He rubbed his hands together. "I sure hope so. I especially like pie."

"Yes… Of course…" She lifted her wrist. "I might be slow about it, but I'd be happy to do some baking."

Kai playfully swatted her dad with a dishtowel and put her arm around Sofia's shoulders protectively. "That's enough. Leave us for a moment." She shooed the men out of the room. "Don't mind them, Sofia. All Mannis men are terrible teases, especially Dad." She pulled out a kitchen chair for Sofia and sat down too. "I'm so glad Jim is home for good this time. And it's so nice you're visiting. Are you glad you're here?" Kai clasped her hands on the table, rubbing one thumb continuously over the other. "That's a silly question. You just got here, so who knows. Well, you will be. I hope. Or, maybe not. I'm not sure."

A tiny laugh sounding more like a contained sneeze escaped Sofia's throat.

"God, I don't know why I'm acting so nervous." Kai burst out laughing.

"I'm nervous too," Sofia said after her own laughter slowed. "This all came about so fast. I feel overwhelmed at the moment. I'm sorry."

Kai reached over and squeezed Sofia's hand. "Don't apologize. Jim filled us in a little and we're here to help. Let's have some breakfast and get you settled. I bet a long nap sounds good. There will be plenty to talk about and show you later."

After breakfast, Sofia opted for staying to chat with Kai as she cleaned up the kitchen. She couldn't offer much beyond a lame attempt at one-handed dish drying, which Kai insisted she found helpful. She tried to avoid glancing at Jim out the kitchen window as he and Leo stood in the driveway talking. The western backdrop fit the man. He took off his hat occasionally to shoo away bugs. When the men turned and Jim smiled her direction through the window, heat crept up her neck. Well aware of Kai observing, she accelerated her drying technique on the dish in front of her.

"Jim told us about the robbery. He mentioned you had a brother who passed away recently. I'm so sorry. I can't imagine how hard that is."

Sofia put a plate on the counter and dabbed at it with a dishtowel to dry it. "Thank you." She inhaled, pain scouring her heart before exhaling.

I will never be Anthony's big sister again. The way Kai is to Jim.

Leo came in the back door, stopping to kiss his wife on the forehead. A moment later, Jim followed. "Sofia, do you want to join me in the living room?"

"Sure, I'll be there in just a minute." She stood next to Kai in front of the sink. "I appreciate your dad letting me stay here. I'm kind of a card-carrying damsel in distress." She glanced Kai's direction, detecting a hint of a smile before Kai's head shot up at a black pickup truck skidding to a stop in front of the house.

"Oh, no." Kai turned off the water and quickly dried her hands. "This doesn't happen often but when it does, it can be ugly. My brother Jett is here. It's better if you go in the living room now."

Jim's sister ushered her through the swinging door to the living room, signaling for Leo to follow her back to the kitchen. Sofia joined Jim on the couch, not interrupting the discussion he and his father were having about a football game coming up later on TV. Without breaking conversation, Jim put his arm on the back of the couch behind her and gave her shoulder a pat.

A deep male voice carried from the kitchen, followed by the bang of the screen door.

"You can't keep me from seeing Dad."

Sofia was accustomed to photographing good-looking actors in her line of work, but none as naturally handsome as the man who entered the living room. He was a leaner version of Jim, over six feet, she'd guess, with chiseled facial features, including incredible cheekbones. The photographer in her visualized a series of black and white photos. She imagined the figure before her on one of the giant digital screens in the city advertising jeans or cologne. Even his name implied a fast-paced image. Jett.

"Dad?" Jett said. "Hey, happy birthday, Dad."

Jim sat forward on the edge of the couch, his hands clasped and jaw visibly tightening. "Dad's birthday was a week ago."

Squatting next to his father's chair, Jett repeated,

"Happy birthday."

She interpreted Ben's dismissive arm gesture as, *go away*. It wasn't like she didn't recognize drunk either. Unsure about whatever dynamic she witnessed, Sofia sat still.

"Damn it, can't you even appreciate that I came to see you on your birthday?"

Jim stood. "Let's go, Jett."

Gripping the arm of his father's chair, Jett awkwardly pushed to stand and swayed. "Big Jim's back." He spread his arms wide. "We're all so lucky to have you here to take care of everything and everyone now, aren't we?" Jett's gaze traveled to Kai and Leo, who both stood, arms crossed next to the kitchen door. When his eyes settled on her, his voice was thick with amusement. "Baby girl."

I can see why Jim took a pass on talking about his brother.

"Excuse me?" She got a whiff of liquor as he moved closer. "My name is Sofia." *Not, baby girl.*

"You. Are. Gorgeous." He put his hand out as if inviting her to depart with him. Staggering, he stepped sideways, laying the same hand over his heart when she didn't accept it. "Where'd you come from, sweetheart?"

"Jett. You're embarrassing yourself. This is a friend of Jim's who's visiting," Kai said.

"Oh, shit." Jett laughed. "You're with Jim?" He shook his head, an expression of disappointment on his face. Coming close again, he touched the cast on her wrist with his fingertips. "What happened to you?"

Jim moved in front of her. "Hands off."

Ben rose from his chair and pushed between his sons. Taking her elbow, he silently led her out of the room and down a hallway.

"I'll help," Kai said from behind as Sofia entered a cozy bedroom with a pretty purple and white quilt she suspected was handmade. After wishing her time to rest, Ben left the room. Kai moved Sofia's bags from the bed to the floor. The curtain at the window breathed in and out with the morning air.

"Give me the keys to your truck and get your ass in the car." The backdoor slammed and Jim's angry voice carried through the open window.

Kai circled the bed and shut the curtain. Exhausted, Sofia didn't have the energy to break the silence. She unzipped her suitcase and pulled out a small toiletry bag.

"I'm just going to say this," Kai said.

Sofia shook her head, already objecting to any apology Kai might offer.

"Please don't hold this awkward moment against Jim."

"I would never think like that. I promise." Sofia folded back the bedspread. "I'm so grateful and just really tired."

"Okay, rest well." Kai told her and closed the door.

She didn't bother to change her clothes, instead slipping under the sheet and then looking around the room. Three small frames hung in a horizontal row on the wall across from her bed. They were watercolor paintings of purple lilacs. Other than the bed and a dresser, the only other furniture was a narrow rocking chair with a high back. Depictions of wildlife—a bear, a wolf, a deer – were carved in the mahogany wood. She closed her eyes and drifted, before a knock brought her awake again.

"Come in."

Jim stuck his head in the door. "You okay? Can I come in?"

"I thought you were long gone." She patted the bed for him to sit.

"We're leaving in a minute. I'm taking Jett home with me. Leo's talking with him so he doesn't do anything else stupid. He's got…issues."

Sofia snuggled further down in the bed. "Let's skip that part."

"What part?"

"Let's skip explaining everyone else for now. Is your father okay?"

"I'll check on him before I leave."

"I'm so worn out. I'm going to go right to sleep in this pretty purple room and wake up to my new adventure where I meet the chickens and the pigs."

Jim chuckled. "Get some rest. I'll come back later for supper."

She listened to every sound as he left. The goodbye to his father. The back door closing. The slam of car doors. The scatter of gravel on the driveway. Then silence settled over her like a weight, comforting in its confinement, and she drifted to sleep.

Chapter 5

JIM HELD ONE ARM AND Leo the other as they dragged his younger brother inside. "Thanks."

"You bet." Leo put a pillow beneath Jett's head. "Kai came over the other day and tried to air out the place. She put fresh sheets on the bed and left some towels."

Jim smiled. "I appreciate it. And that you two have taken care of this old house. It's pretty convenient having a home of my own to come to."

"It's part of the property with the lodge." Leo shrugged. "Do you want to check out the lodge now or should I take off so you can catch some shut-eye?"

Glancing at the snoring body on the couch, Jim sighed. "Let's go now. If I go to sleep, I won't get up until noon tomorrow, and I promised Sofia I'd be back at Dad's for supper."

"She seems like a nice woman. Not hard to look at either, but don't tell your sister I said that. It must be pretty weird for her, coming here."

"Yeah. I'm a little worried about how it's all going to go. She has a broken wrist and probably PTSD from being at the scene of a bank robbery and seeing two men shot."

"What about you, you okay?" Leo asked.

"I'm fine," Jim said.

"You could have her make an appointment with Cindy Wheeler. Maybe having someone to talk to about everything would be helpful."

"God, I forgot about Doc Cindy moving her practice here from Utah. Good idea. I'll bring it up to Sofia when the timing is right. Do you remember my buddy, Rafe?"

"Of course."

"He has a huge crush on Doc Cindy."

"When did he meet her?"

"Never has. Kai sent me a copy of her first book. He saw her photo on the back. Read it cover to cover. Boom. Instant love."

Leo smirked. "That would definitely be a case of opposites attract. I can't picture it."

After driving the mile from the house to Mercy Mountain Lodge, Leo handed him the keys. Jim unlocked the door and stepped inside. A streak of sunshine swept across the bare room, dust particles dancing in the light.

"Whoo wee." Leo waved his hat in front of his face. "That's musty."

Jim walked the entire main room, the sound of his boots echoing off the wood floor. He took his time, listening to his brother-in-law's steps in nearby rooms. A familiar creak of the floor brought memories of running around the lodge that served as his late mother's art studio. A wave of nostalgia hit him as he pictured her working on one of her sculptures. She'd turn her bright eyes whenever he entered the room. Any room. God, he missed her. Missed the way she loved him. How she loved all of them. Longing must have shown on his sleeve, because Leo walked toward him and put a hand on his shoulder.

"I'm glad you're home, man. You've made Kai very happy, and you know if your sister is happy, everybody's happy,"

"That's good." Jim nodded, letting his eyes sweep over the room again. "This could be nice in winter." He walked toward the old fireplace – a vision forming in his mind of the glow of a fire, a nice leather couch and Sofia, with her legs curled up, a soft blanket around her shoulders.

"Your dad came by here the other day."

Leo's words brought him out of his daydream. "Yeah?"

"First time, he said, in twenty-something years. Hard to believe it's been closed up for so long. Jett's helped maintain it too, not just us."

"Jett?" His suspicions aroused at the mention of his younger brother. "Did he make Dad pay him to do that?"

"No, but he never turns down cash from Kai. There's no shortage of women wanting to baby him," Leo added. "First in line is your older sister and my wife, no matter how annoyed she acts."

"So, how's he really doing? Is what I saw today typical?"

Leo moved to the fireplace and ran his finger

along a hairline crack running from the mantel up the wall toward the ceiling. "Not always. We don't see him much. He gets periodic construction work and that keeps him going, I guess. He usually has some pretty young thing on his arm, if he does come by. Never the same one. I don't think it takes even the dumb ones long to realize it'll take more than an amazing fuck to cure his drinking problem." Leo grinned his direction. "But with his looks, they sure are willing to try."

Jim didn't answer, walking the room again, stopping to gaze out the row of windows to the west toward the majesty of Mercy Mountain. A low stretch of foothills, Moonshine Ridge, was his favorite. As a boy, he imagined a fortress surrounding his land. The sea lay beyond the hills in his fantasy. Intense battles raged on those imaginary waters, with Jim as a great commander. In reality, there was no ocean within hundreds of miles.

"Did he know I was coming back now?"

"Jett? Oh, yeah."

Leo's long-suffering tone made Jim glance at him. "That bad?"

"You left when your brother was twelve years old. How many times have you been home in the last, what, eighteen years?"

"And he knows I'm moving into the house on the property?" Jim grunted. "I guess he will when he wakes up there."

Leo grimaced as if speaking with the sorriest son of a bitch alive. "Jett thinks he knows *everything*. The war veteran and hero cop returns to the cheers of the local community and takes over the castle. That's you."

"What does he expect? Dad would never put him in charge of renovating the lodge. But bottom line, it belongs to Kai and you, me, and Jett.

"This place is a dump. No offense to your late mother. It's going to be a hell of a job trying to bring it back. Here you are, like the prodigal son returning and you get the golden goose too."

Jim flipped the lock on the sliding glass door leading to a back deck. "You seem to be combining a number of stories."

Leo snorted a laugh and followed him outside. "I was never good with my Bible stories. Or Mother Goose or whatever."

"What about you and Kai?" He put his hands on the dilapidated wood railing, careful to avoid getting a splinter, or in case the damn thing decided to crumble.

"We're good." Leo walked the deck, kicking a couple buckets left in a corner with his foot. "We trust whatever you have in mind. You know, with our jobs at the clinic, we won't have much time to offer. Kai understands that may mean she gets less of a cut if there's ever a sale or you keep the property and there's a profit someday."

Jim turned. "I'd never do that. You're the ones that have been here all along. It's a third each. Besides, you got all those mouths to feed at your place. How are all my nieces and nephews doing by the way?"

"Our house is a zoo." Leo counted off on his fingers. "Teenage boy and girl. Both are nightmares, by the way. The twins start second grade in the fall. And Suze. They can't wait to see you. The girls are going to be excited about someone like Sofia being around. Do you know if she likes kids?"

He thought about his stupid question on the airplane about whether she wanted kids. "I hardly know her. She recently lost a younger brother to cancer. That was her only sibling."

"Oh, shit," Leo said. "I'm sorry to hear that. Maybe we better ease into the family thing then. The whole crew can be overwhelming and if she's not used to a kid with Downs, like Suze, it could be too much.

"My girl, Suze." Jim smiled. "I've missed that little munchkin. Are pink and purple still her favorite colors?"

Leo scoffed. "Are you kidding? She amazes Kai and me. All the others are tomboys regardless of gender. You know, dirt-bike, rock-climbing, fishing-crazy maniacs. Then there's Suze with her frilly dresses and stuffed animals." Leo shook his head. "Her latest thing is taking notes in these little tiny notebooks. Pink of course. And she has purple pens with streamers hanging off the ends of them too."

Jim laughed and gestured for them to head back inside. "It's good to be home."

The aroma of fresh coffee woke Sofia, and she breathed deeply in pure pleasure opening her eyes. The sun shone brightly through the window and across the bed. It took a moment to realize she wasn't in New York and a double take at the clock on the nightstand to register it was ten in the morning.

I can't believe I slept so late.

She pulled a pair of yoga pants and socks from her suitcase, then sat on the edge of the bed to put her clothes on with her one working hand. Her stomach growled as she padded down the hall.

I don't even remember anyone trying to wake me for supper.

Ben sat at the kitchen table reading a newspaper, several sections piled on the table in front of him. His pressed shirt and crisp slacks gave her the impression he'd been up and active for several hours. He smiled, gesturing for her to sit. "Good morning. Coffee?"

Sofia nodded, accepting the mug Ben fetched for her. "Good morning. I guess I was totally out last night."

"We decided not to wake you." Ben smiled. "I bet you're starving." He pushed a neatly arranged plate with cinnamon rolls and butter on the side toward her. "Help yourself."

She ran a shaky hand through her hair. "Thank you."

"Leo will be here in about an hour to drive Jett's truck over to Jim's house, if you want to tag along."

Sofia hesitated. "I'd like that."

"You don't need to worry about Jett. He rarely shows up and when he does, he clears out again in a hurry. He drinks too much," Ben said matter of fact. "It's a shame that's the state he was in, your first day here. We do what we can to sober him up, even if it's just overnight." Ben paused. "He was nine when the kids' mother died. He has struggled one way or another ever since."

"I'm sorry, that must be very hard to lose your mother so young." Sofia added cream to her coffee and stirred. "May I ask –?"

"Catherine had breast cancer. It was six months from diagnosis to the end. She was an artist and a wonderful mother. Loving and strong. Just not here as long as we all would have liked." Ben got up and brought the coffee pot to the table, refilling his mug. "Jim told me your brother passed away recently. I'm sorry to hear that. Would you tell me something about him?"

Sofia took a bite of her roll and contemplated how to begin. "Anthony is…was… four years younger than me. He had cancer too. Adult onset leukemia. He passed away in June."

"That's how he died. How did Anthony live?"

The care in Ben's manner and the direct question put her at ease. Most people asked if she was okay, but she sensed they didn't want to hear more than how she was hanging in there. "Okay, well, we grew up on Staten Island. In the summers, we ran barefoot outside and climbed trees. We rode our bikes everywhere." Sofia took another sip of her coffee. "That's not how people usually think of New York. It was rare for us to go to the city, but when we did we took the ferry. We'd race from one end of the boat to the other."

She smiled at Ben's encouraging nod. "Anthony coached high school football. It was his dream job. He had a nice girlfriend."

"You loved him and he loved you."

"Yes." Her voice choked.

"It's good to be loved, even better to love back."

She stared into her coffee mug, lost in a vision of her and Anthony sitting at a picnic table in the backyard surrounded by family. *Was it the Fourth of July or one of the cousins' graduation parties?*

Ben patted her arm. "How about you tell me something more about Anthony tomorrow?"

His look invited a response, so she agreed.

"Good. I'll look forward to hearing more about him."

After breakfast, Sofia took a shower with her left arm wrapped in a garbage bag. She managed to get her underwear and jeans on one-handed before the back door slammed.

"Sofia?"

Crap. Leo.

Unable to button her pants, she fumbled with her front clasping bra and scrambled into a t-shirt.

I cannot show up at Jim's house with my pants undone.

She cracked the bathroom door, leaning her forehead against it. "I'm in the bathroom. I…I need some help, please."

Purposeful footsteps moved down the hall. She hid behind the door, peeking out at Leo.

"Well, you're standing up," Leo said. "So I guess

you don't need help wiping."

"What? No!"

"You know I'm a nurse, right? I've seen and done it all."

Her cheeks heated. "I can't button my jeans."

Leo let out a hearty laugh. "Hell, that's no big deal. Let's get your pants fastened."

She held the door a moment longer, then let go, facing him. Leo pulled her pants waist tight, then buttoned them.

"There." He pointed to a short sleeve red hoodie sitting on top of the toilet seat. "Let's get that on too." He helped her put her head through, first one arm, then the other, stretching the sleeve over her cast. "Now we mussed up your hair." His hands on her shoulders he turned her to the mirror. Handing her the brush, he moved to the hallway. "Grab your stuff when you're ready. Meet me in the driveway."

Sofia hurried to follow, stopping to get her camera case and sunglasses off the bed. She didn't question Leo when he told her not to bother with the lock on the backdoor.

The old pickup truck wasn't in the driveway. "Is Ben gone?"

"Yes, he always goes to the senior center on Saturday or Sunday. All the ladies are there on the weekends, plus dessert. You'll soon learn that the Mannis men, or in my case, McCreed, never miss out on a chance to hang with the ladies or eat sweets."

"It's been mentioned that pie is a favorite."

Leo gently supported her by the elbow to help her into the truck and chuckled. "That's right."

Chapter 6

THE SMELL OF PINE TREES grew strong as they passed the Little Forest Fairgrounds and turned onto a dirt road. The tree-lined drive led toward a large two-story home with black window sills. A decorative arch looked like it led to a secret garden. The backdrop to the house was foothills and in the far distance, snow-covered mountains.

"No shirt, no shoes, no service." Leo pointed through the windshield to where Jett sat on the front stoop. Barefoot and shirtless, he held a coffee mug in his hand. After pulling to a stop, Leo reached over to release her seatbelt. She liked his low-key, no-nonsense approach to helping her.

He got out of the truck, directing a shout toward Jett. "Hey, fresh start! I brought someone you can apologize to and then you're giving me a ride back." He bounded up the steps to Jim's house, slapping Jim's brother hard on his bare back before entering.

Sofia took her time, gathering her camera and

her nerves before walking toward the house. She stopped about three feet before Jett. Good looking and young enough, any effects from his alcohol abuse weren't noticeable. She managed to snap a one-handed picture of him before he put a hand up blocking his face.

"The morning after." She sat down next to him. "Where's Jim?"

"Taking a shower." He glanced at her. "Better not let him catch you sitting by me."

"Hmm, thing is, I sit wherever I like." Sofia smiled. "Are you afraid for me or for yourself?"

He took a swig of his coffee and leaned back, elbows resting on the step behind him. "Most definitely me. Listen, I'm sorry. I don't know you at all, but I wasn't on my best behavior last night. Or so I've been told."

Sofia nodded. "Drinking can do that to a person."

"It won't happen again, baby girl."

She lifted her chin. "My name is Sofia, not baby girl. Can I ask you something?"

"Shoot."

"Do you need a friend?"

"Huh?"

"Forget it." She studied her shoes intently. "It's nothing."

Jett sat up, resting his forearms on his knees. "Why'd you ask me that?"

"I just thought you might need someone to listen."

"Do you?"

"Me?" She swallowed at the fluttery sound of

her own voice.

"Yeah, you, baby… Sofia." He drew her name out slowly. "Do you need someone to listen? Jim told me the bare minimum about why you're here. About the robbery."

She glanced away, rattled a bit by the way he studied her face. "Your brother shot the gunman. He saved my life."

"Ahh." He nodded. "I get it. Big Jim…the hero. Kind of makes you feel like you have to live up to his expectations, doesn't it?"

I don't know what he expects of me. Maybe to stay out of his way?

"It's not like that."

"Whatever you say." Jett took a gulp of his coffee. "Tell me about this friend offer."

She shrugged. "No judgment. Just listening. Or if you need a ride somewhere. I can drive one-handed if it's not a stick."

"Rides, huh? So as my friend, you would get the honor of chauffeuring me around. What kind of stuff do I get to do for you?"

She felt heat creep across her cheeks. Taking a chance, she bumped his shoulder playfully.

"Hey!" he said when coffee sloshed from his mug.

"Oh, crap, I'm sorry."

Jett shook his wet hand and wiped it on his jeans. "I see how this friendship is going to go." He put out his hand, a light squeeze to his handshake. "Friends."

"Friends with rides." She stood. "I think I'll go inside now."

When she turned to the steps, Jim was leaning against the frame inside the screen door, his arms crossed. "Good morning."

"Good morning. How long have you been standing there?"

He pushed the screen door open, holding it with his foot. "Long enough." She passed by, flinching as the door slammed behind her. "Come into the kitchen. Leo's getting ready to leave and he's taking the hound dog you were making friends with home."

"Bet you never imagined you'd be basically surrounded by all men during your visit, did you?" Leo said.

She glanced at Leo sitting at the kitchen table, chuckling and blowing on his coffee before taking a sip. She considered Jim, leaning nonchalantly against the counter, and not to forget Jett, who called her baby girl again on the porch steps.

Yep. There's a lot of manliness going on right here.

Resting her cast on her hip, she tilted her head to one side and faced Jim. "Oh, I don't know, men can be handy. For example, Leo helped me button and zip my pants this morning."

He stalked two steps her direction, put his hands on her shoulders and gently moved her to the side. "Say, what?" he asked Leo.

"I *am* a medical professional. She has a broken wrist."

Sofia gave as wide-eyed and innocent a look as possible without laughing. "Quite chivalrous, if you ask me."

"And on that note…adios." Leo got up with

Jim following close behind as he left the room.

The screen door slammed. "Thanks *Nurse* Leo."

Sofia leaned around the corner looking at Jim's authoritative stance as he stood guard at the back door.

"You got yourself one sexy, tough girl," Jett called from outside. "She says she's my friend and she's going to drive me around town."

Jim's head shot up. "Shut up, Jett."

Sofia bit her lip. It was like she'd written a script and Jett delivered his ridiculous lines perfectly.

"Oh, come on. I didn't mean anything."

"Skip it." Jim slammed the back door and turned around.

Covering her mouth with her hand, she tried not to laugh when he caught her peeking. "I was teasing all of you. You know," she backed up as she spoke, watching the slow-growing smile on his face as he walked down the hall, "dissipating the dude vibe…all that testosterone."

A zing of flirty energy shot up her spine when he stopped in front of her and tugged on the drawstring of her red sweatshirt.

"Very clever, little red riding hood."

He headed into the kitchen. "I'm going to make myself some lunch. Are you hungry?"

She took a seat at the table. "No, thanks. I had a late breakfast at your dad's."

"What would you like to do today?" He spoke while taking out sandwich makings from the fridge. "Want to take a drive? We could head up to the mountains." Jim put a bottle of water in front of her, then picked it up again and twisted the top open. "Any headaches? Drink lots of water. It's the best thing for adjusting to the elevation here."

"A drive sounds nice. But I don't want you to feel like you have to entertain me."

"I'd like to go. I don't have any plans until tomorrow."

She took a sip and glanced around the barren kitchen. "So, was this your house before you lived in New York?"

"No." He spread mustard on a piece of bread. "This house and the lodge about a mile from here are property my mother bought a long time ago. At one point, my grandmother on my mom's side lived in this house for a few years after my grandfather died. I don't remember that or her very well. I was pretty little." Jim paused, putting his sandwich together, and then sat down at the table. "My mom used the lodge as her art studio." He spoke around a bite. "She was a sculptress."

"Wow. Are her sculptures in any museums?"

"Not that I know of. There are several around Ashnee Valley. I guess you could say she was a famous local artist. She had more sculptures finished when she died, but they were never placed anywhere. They're in the basement of the lodge."

"Really? I'd love to see them. And this is the lodge you're going to renovate?"

"Yup."

"Your dad told me your mom died when Jett was about nine. How old were you?"

"Fifteen."

She took another sip of water and didn't ask

more questions as he finished his lunch.

He spun a finger at her. "I see the wheels turning in there. Trying to piece it together." He smiled, picked up his plate, and walked to the counter.

It seemed easier to admit he was correct with his back to her. "Maybe."

After rinsing his plate, he turned. "We all fell apart when Mom died. Dad, especially. It seems I've never lived up to his expectation to look after Jett the way he did for his younger brothers. Both his parents died when he was twenty and my uncles weren't even teenagers yet."

"So young."

"I started vandalizing shit…" He shook his head. "Blowing off steam, I guess. Doing stupid stuff, like spray-painting buildings. I somehow graduated from high school, then signed up with the Army the day I turned eighteen. After three tours in Afghanistan I left and joined the police force." He dried his hands on a dishtowel and leaned against the counter. "Your turn."

Sofia lowered her chin. "You know most of my story. I'm a photographer. Or I was before I got fired. My brother died a few months ago. I left my psychiatrist's office and walked right into the middle of a bank robbery. From there, I became an overnight media sensation complete with death threats. So I ran away in the middle of the night to Colorado."

"You were fired? When?"

She sighed. "The day we left." She finished the last swallow from her bottle. "I'll take another, if you have one."

Jim opened the fridge and handed her more water. "Did you get fired because of coming here?"

"Mmm, not entirely for that reason. I've been struggling since Anthony died. And I…"

Do not tell him you slept with your boss. He'll think you are A, a moron. B, a hussy.

"And you…?"

"What day is it?" she blurted.

"Saturday."

"Oh, shoot. Dr. Platt. I had an appointment with her for yesterday. I didn't even call her to say I was leaving."

"That's your psychiatrist?"

C, a crazy woman.

"Yes." Sofia inhaled and opened her eyes again. "Could we go back to the part in your story where you started vandalizing buildings. Because I would feel better about myself if you shared more about that."

He scratched his chin and chuckled. "You have a good sense of humor. What do you say we table all stories for now and head out for a drive?"

"Great idea."

"Hey, I'm sorry you got fired."

"That makes two of us."

She woke up with a jolt from a dream where she missed a step and thought she was falling. Out the truck window she faced a wall of rock as they wound their way through a canyon. She covered a yawn with the back of her hand and sat up.

He took his eyes off the road and glanced her direction. "Welcome back."

"Did I conk out? That's embarrassing."

"You were sawing some serious logs, that's for sure."

"I was not." She wrinkled her nose. "Did I snore?"

He shook his head, his eyes back on the road. "I'm kidding."

"This is beautiful. Where are we?"

"Darkhorse Canyon. That's the Talking Fish River." He pointed out her side of the car. "It runs right through the center of Ashnee Valley. You'll see it when you're in town."

Sofia rolled down her window, letting the warm breeze caress her face. "It smells amazing here. The air. The sunshine." She closed her eyes and took a deep breath. "I guess sunshine can't have a smell."

"Sure, it can. You can think whatever you want here."

His words sounded like permission. To be anonymous. To have no past. No future. Just float. The road and blue sky opened up as they came out of the canyon. The few clouds were oblong and smooth, like flying saucers hovering.

A person could disappear here. Just wander up one of these hills and keep on walking.

"While you were sleeping, I thought more about the fact that you were fired."

Jim's voice jarred her back to reality. "It's my fault." She waved her cast. "Don't worry about it. My old boss said I could call him when I return." She lay her head back. "I've decided to give up my apartment in the city. That will get rid of one expense. I can arrange all that from here. I'll move home or at least move closer to my parents. They'll need me now that I'm the one left. Anyway, I have a couple weeks to get my act together."

"Won't your cast be on longer than two weeks?"

"I didn't think about that." She sighed. "But whatever."

"I have an idea."

She stiffened in her seat as he pulled the car to the side of the road and put it in park.

"You could stay here longer."

She swallowed. "Longer?"

"I could use some help with getting renovations started at the lodge. Jett is the one with construction experience, but we aren't on solid ground. Plus, I won't be able to be two places at once. Dad's older now. It does help if you're staying with him. Maybe that's mainly for my peace of mind."

She studied his eager expression unsure why he came across sincere—but a scant desperate-car-salesman too.

"If you're thinking I'm saying all this because I feel sorry for you," he added with a straight face, "I am."

His teasing made her laugh. "What kind of stuff would I do?"

"Some errands around town and phone calls. There are permits and contractors to gather bids from. My buddy Rafe is coming soon, but he won't be here for another week. When he does arrive, we'll start hiring more guys. I'd pay you, of course."

"That won't be necessary. I'm staying at your dad's house, eating your food... maybe driving Jett around town." Her snicker stopped short at the glower on his face.

"No Jett."

"I'm kidding. Your brother won't be asking me for any rides."

"No Jett. Anything. Ever. Period."

Sofia silently counted to ten and let out a puff of air. "Sorry, no deal then."

He whipped off his sunglasses. "Excuse me?"

"I'm not saying no to everything, okay? I want to help. And I'll think more about it. It's a generous offer." She paused. "But. Just like I told Jett not to call me baby girl this morning, I'm telling you not to say who I can or can't spend time with."

Jim hung his head and groaned. "Sofia."

"I'm not going to seek him out. I promise."

Putting the truck in drive, he pulled back on the road. "It's not you I'm worried about doing the seeking."

Chapter 7

IT WAS FIVE DAYS SINCE his drive in the mountains with Sofia. Jim spent time unpacking after movers arrived with his furniture and other belongings from New York. Plus he had a new truck, a welcome return to having his own transportation. A trip to the grocery store that morning provided him with more options than the ham sandwiches he'd been eating.

Kai followed him so he could drop off the rental vehicle, and by late afternoon, he was taking her home before heading to his dad's house.

"Did you happen to see Sofia yesterday?" he asked his sister.

"No. I called her to ask if she needed anything because Dad was going to be at church and the senior center most of the day. She was tired and planning to call home." Kai smiled. "I think she wanted some alone time."

"I asked her to stay longer. To help me get started with the lodge. Do some administrative stuff." He pulled into Kai's driveway. "Are the kids around? I could say hello for a second."

Kai got out and walked around to the driver side window. "It's pizza day. I'm meeting everyone downtown." She jiggled her keys at him. "How about a cookout this weekend? When does Rafe get here?"

"Saturday."

"Leo and I both work Saturday. How about Sunday? The whole crowd."

Jim rubbed the back of his neck. "Sure, I could ask Sofia if she'd be up for it."

Kai grinned. "It's nice the way you look out for her."

Jim put his hand up. "Don't start."

"You like her."

He dropped his head back in frustration. "There are a million reasons why I am not going down that road, so you can wipe that goofy look off your face. She's here for a few weeks is one."

"You just asked her to stay longer. That must mean —"

"Stop." Jim laughed. "She's got her own plans for getting back to New York. I'm not taking advantage of a grieving woman, either."

Kai hugged him through the window. "Darn your nobility."

It took him all of eight minutes to get from his sister's place to the ranch. He'd forgotten how close everything was in Ashnee Valley compared to maneuvering around New York. He parked his truck next to his dad's and looked through the windshield at the smaller of the two barns. It was used as a storage building most of the time when he was a kid. A place where art supplies were delivered for his mom. For all he knew the dirt bikes he, Jett, and Kai used to ride were still in there. *I was in such a hurry to leave this place. To leave home.* He got out of the truck, paused to consider whether to take peek in the barn, decided against it, and headed toward the house.

"Dad?" he called as he opened the door, his voice booming through the small kitchen before he saw his father sitting at the table.

"Shhh. Sofia is napping."

"Sorry." Jim tip-toed into the room.

Ben put his book down. "Son, you can walk normal. Just don't talk so loud."

"Right." He got a glass from the cupboard, filled it at the sink, and sat down. "I wanted to talk with you about a few things related to the lodge. I asked Sofia to stay a few weeks longer and help me. I should have talked to you first. Is that going to be a problem?"

"Not at all," Ben answered. "I'm enjoying having her here. Although I did make her cry this morning."

"What'd you do that for?" He scooted his chair back and headed down the hall toward the bedrooms. Carefully opening the door, he stuck his head in to confirm she was still asleep. Curtains closed, the room semi-dark, she faced the other direction, lying on her side. He slipped into the room and put an afghan from the rocking chair over her, closed the door, and went back to the kitchen.

"I didn't do it on purpose…exactly," Ben said.

Jim sat down again. "Start at the beginning. How did Sunday go?"

"Good. I went to church and then the senior center. They had chocolate cream pie."

"I meant how did Sunday go for Sofia?"

"Fine. She sleeps a lot. She mentioned she called home and misses her mom and her friend."

"I bet."

"She's been through a lot. Who can blame her?"

"What happened this morning?"

"I thought maybe some good old-fashioned outdoor work, like gardening, would be a healthy thing." Ben pulled at his shirt collar. "She's been telling me a little bit about her brother each day."

"Dad. She has a broken wrist."

"It wasn't about the gardening. I thought it would be a way to coax more out of her. She's so quiet. It's all bottled up in her. I know a little bit about grief, you know."

"I know you do." Jim waited for his father to continue.

"We wrapped her arm in a plastic bag. That way she wouldn't get her cast dirty. I showed her how to feed the chickens. Then we worked in the vegetable garden together. She asked me why dirt smelled so good." Ben chuckled. "I asked her to tell me something more about Anthony. Has she told you much about her family?"

He shook his head. "I met her parents in New York. They're nice people. Sofia looks just like her mother."

"She's from a good family, big with all the grandparents, uncles and aunts and cousins always around. Even so, she and her brother and parents, they were like a tight little unit, especially on Christmas mornings." Ben took a kerchief out of his back pocket and wiped his eyes. "Just the four of them."

Jim swallowed the lump in his throat. "Are you sure you made her cry and not the other way around?"

Ben blew his nose and laughed. "You wait until you're as old as me. Tears come easy. It reminded me of the five of us before your mother died. A family can disburse and you'd give anything to get that tightness back."

Jim put a hand on his father's shoulder when his chin quivered. "I'm not going anywhere."

"Good." Ben cleared his throat. "I think Sofia enjoys telling me about Anthony's antics. How they'd race to the Christmas tree when their parents gave them the go. She'd let him win every time. He'd unwrap his presents in a frenzy, where she's more cautious." Ben tapped his fingers on the table. "It got to be around lunch time, so we headed to the barn to store the tools. We were standing in front of the washbasin side-by-side. Her hand was black with dirt. I don't know why I didn't give her a glove. Anyway, I held her hand beneath the water and soaped it with my own. I could tell she was crying, without even looking at her. So I dried her hand and put my arm around her."

"And you said what Mom used to say."

Ben nodded. "Weeding. It makes space for new dreams to grow."

Jim blew out a breath. "We're not exactly the poster family for dealing with our emotions. Is that why renovating the lodge is so important to you?"

"I want it to be something you all contribute to. The ranch has never been that. I want the lodge to bring the three of you kids together again."

"You know Jett will want to fix it up and flip it."

"That's why you're in charge. It stays in the family."

Jim sighed. "Sofia's been seeing a doctor in New York, a psychiatrist. I'm going to mention Cindy Wheeler. Maybe she'd want to talk to her."

"That's a good idea."

Thirty minutes later, his dad left for his Monday night card game. Jim stood at the stove, re-heating soup he'd picked up from Patsy's Diner on the way over. He set the timer on the oven to warm homemade rolls his sister stocked in the freezer for his dad. Daydreaming, he stirred and pictured Sofia stretched out on the bed with him. Her hair draped across his chest as she descended with light kisses. His ever-growing hard on made him feel like a teenager.

"Whatcha doing?"

Soup splashed on his hand when he dropped the spoon. "Ouch."

She gave him a sympathetic look, walked to the stove, and peered in the pot. "Are you making soup?"

"Yes, and bread."

"What time is it? Did you father already leave for his card game?"

"It's five-thirty."

"You're kidding. I've been asleep over four hours. Was your dad upset? We were going to take the horse out."

The crease on her cheek left behind by heavy sleep, combined with mussed up hair, made him smile. "He gave strict instructions to let you sleep as long as you needed. You can help me brush the horse after supper." He moved around the room, pulling bowls and glasses from the cupboards. "Can you stir the soup while I set the table?"

"Sure." Sofia moved to the stove. "This is nice, just you and me."

A minute later, he rested his hands lightly on her hips, turning her toward the table. "Sit." He ladled the soup to her first, then himself, and poured two glasses of milk. He caught her watching him as he worked. After putting the pan in the sink, he sat at the table. Lifting a spoonful of soup, he blew on it, looking across the table at her.

"You're smiling at me funny. What?" Sofia asked.

"Nothing."

"Tell me. Do I look weird?" Her cheeks flushed with color. "Bedhead? What?"

"You look fine. You have beautiful hair." Jim put his spoon in his bowl without taking a bite. "Did you decide about staying longer?"

She pulled her roll apart and dipped a piece in the butter on her plate. "Yes, I'd like to stay.

Especially since I talked to my folks yesterday and I'm still on the media marquee. Where has slutty Nurse Nightingale disappeared to?"

He smirked. "No one called you slutty. Did they?"

"Have you ever been on social media?"

He resumed eating. "Don't look at that crap. People are cruel. I thought we'd get started tomorrow on the lodge."

"Sounds good."

"Speaking of people, I wanted to mention someone you might enjoy meeting."

"Like a friend of yours?"

"Not exactly."

"A contractor for the lodge?"

"No."

She frowned, looking up from her soup. "Who do you want me to meet?"

"It's a doctor, like the one you had in New York. She's local. Her name is Cindy Wheeler. Her dad, Brady Wheeler, was my dad's best friend. They grew up together here. Anyway, Brady died a couple years ago. Cindy is his youngest."

"I take it your dad told you I cried gardening today?"

"Actually, he cried while telling me about you crying. It wasn't easy, but I somehow managed not to cry myself."

She burst out laughing. "You make me laugh, Jim. I forget to be depressed for a few seconds."

"I'm glad." He smiled, taking another roll and dipping it in the last of his soup. "Doc Wheeler's sister died when she was five. When *they* were five. She's a twin. I don't know if that feels the same as something like your situation…"

"I can still talk to Dr. Platt by phone. It's not the same as in person, I guess." She stood, taking her bowl to the sink. "I'll think about it."

Jim cleared the table, bringing the rest of the dishes to the counter. "Let's leave cleanup for later and go to the barn."

Outside, he stood at the fence while Sofia grabbed her jacket inside. When she arrived, he helped her get the sleeve of the windbreaker over her cast. His dad's ancient horse walked around the far side of the corral, bending occasionally to nibble on scattered tufts of grass. Jim reached in his pocket and pulled out a small plastic bag containing several apple slices. The horse lifted its head and trotted over.

Sofia stepped back as the horse approached. "It's like a dinner bell."

"Don't be scared. You're going to feed her the apple so she gets to know you better. Move back up."

"That's okay, I'll watch you. I'll learn now and do it tomorrow. Or never."

"Nice try," Jim said. "Here, I'll show you. Make your hand flat and hold your thumb in, don't let it stick out or she might bite it." He held her hand and put an apple piece in the middle of her palm. "Go ahead and offer it. She'll take it."

He stood behind her as she fed the horse several pieces of apple. She backed up, bumping against him when the horse nudged closer. "She's happy, she wants to get closer to you."

He reached past Sofia and ran his hand down the center of the animal's head. Then took her hand and ran it along the same path. "Come on, let's take her in the stable."

After another twenty minutes guiding Sofia through brushing the horse, he led the way back to the house.

Inside, she washed her hand, then stretched her arms above her head, clasping her hand and cast together.

"Tired?"

"Hard to believe after a long nap, I know."

"Why don't you take it easy." He gestured toward the living room. "I'll put the dishes in the dishwasher and join you in a minute."

"Next time I'll clean up after supper."

"Deal."

A few minutes later, he found her curled up on the couch, listening to his dad's favorite radio station. Country classic WXCZ. "Do you like this music?"

"It's growing on me. I listened to it yesterday. I like the storytelling. I know a few songs, like some Johnny Cash and Willie Nelson."

"Do you want to dance?"

She uncurled her legs and put her feet on the floor and stared at him. "Not a single man," she said, emphasizing each word by slashing her hand through the air, "in my family, dances. Wait, that's not true. Voluntarily. If forced at a wedding, then yes. Like father of the bride stuff. But that's it."

He flashed a lopsided grin. "So, no?"

Sofia stood. "Are you kidding? Yes, I want to dance."

"Do you know how?" He kept a straight face in response to her glare. "Because if not, you could stand on my feet and I'll try to teach you."

Rolling her eyes, she stepped close and clunked her cast on his chest and put her other hand out. He immediately struggled with finding a way to move to the accelerated beat of the song currently playing.

"I thought you could dance."

"You're the one staring at your feet the whole time."

"You're huge. If you step on my foot, I'll never walk again."

He pulled them to a stop. "This song is about to end. Let's see if the next one is slower." He didn't move his hand from her hip as they stood staring at each other.

"Well, this isn't awkward at all." She laughed.

"Have patience, this will be good." He listened to the first few bars of the next song. It was familiar...

Oh, shit. Of course. That corny song about a woman who makes a guy glad he's a man when they're in the sack.

Her forehead rested on his chest as she shook with laughter.

"No laughing," he said, even though he did too. "Listen to the words. She's always a lady."

Sofia snorted.

"That's not very ladylike."

When the song ended, she stepped back, taking her cast off his shoulder and let go his other hand.

"Had enough?" He sucked in a breath when she moved close again, her eyes steady on his.

"I know this song. It's romantic." She wrapped her arms around his middle. "I promise not to make any untoward moves on you."

Nice. Kissing distance. All I'd have to do is dip my head.

At the sound of the back door opening, he repressed a groan, stepped away and turned off the radio.

What idiot had the bright idea to have her stay here instead of my house?

Chapter 8

FOR HER FIRST DAY OF working on the lodge, Sofia made herself wear jeans and a button -down shirt with a collar instead of the yoga pants and t-shirts she'd been sporting around Ben's house. The bathroom didn't have a scale, or she would have weighed herself. Her jeans were looser than she remembered. As if confirming food wasn't much interest, she accepted Ben's offer of coffee when she entered the kitchen but declined breakfast.

"What kind of things are you and Jim doing today?" Ben asked.

"I'm not sure. Maybe making some phone calls. I'm excited to see the lodge though. I've heard about how it was Catherine's studio and some of her sculptures are still in the basement."

Ben held up his finger as the crunch of tires on gravel filled the air. "That's Jim. Maybe I'll stop by this afternoon."

"That'd be great. See you later." Sofia pulled the strap of her camera bag onto her shoulder and headed outside.

Jim came around and opened the door of his truck. "Morning."

"Good morning." Sofia climbed in. "I love this new truck smell," she added when he got in.

"It smells a lot better than the lodge, fair warning. It's been closed up so it's dusty, and there's a mildew issue."

"Gross. Well, that's why you have to fix it up. I brought my camera, so I can take some pictures."

He put the truck in drive. "It would be cool to have some before, during, and after photos."

"I may not be here for much of the during and after, but I can get you started on before. What's the plan for today?"

He checked both directions at the end of the drive and pulled onto the main road. "We're going to ease into it. There are two inspectors coming and some other guy who wants me to drive him around the entire acreage. It's all related to permits. There's an upstairs in the lodge that was never used when my mother was alive. I want to check that out to see what shape it's in. I don't recall how many rooms are up there, maybe eight. Oh, and I asked a couple contractors to come out and look at the foundation so I can get quotes."

"That's easing into things?" Sofia laughed. "What do you want me to do?"

"Since I don't know when each guy will arrive, I thought you could be available in case I'm driving the property or finishing up with one when another arrives."

"So, kind of run interference?"

"Yes. But now that I'm thinking about it more, having you take photos of everything inside and out is a great idea. Not just for capturing the transformation, but I can do some research, talk to people online, and have your photos to work with." He glanced her direction. "Is that boring, asking you to do the thing you always do?"

"Photography? Not at all. I'm glad I can be useful. Tomorrow, I'll bring my tripod. I might be a little limited today with the whole one-handed thing."

Jim made a turn and the road climbed. The trees grew in size and density. Her ears popped.

"If you get tired today, your hand or otherwise, don't sweat it. Just take a break whenever you want. There's a nice deck if the dust gets to be too much." Jim gestured like he erased a blackboard. "Except for the railing, which is rotted. Maybe that's not so safe right now."

"I'll be fine," Sofia said as the road twisted, went back downhill again, and they crossed a bridge over the river. "Is that the Talking Fish River still?"

"Yes, it's the only river to speak of around here. This is the area where the flooding was the worst in seventy-seven." Jim pointed. "Right there is where the Wheelers' car went over into the water and they lost Doc Wheeler's twin sister, who I mentioned to you."

"I can't imagine. The bridge looks so sturdy."

"In those days it wasn't built from steel."

"I have been thinking about your suggestion to speak with her. It takes some time to build trust with a new doctor. I haven't decided. I did email Dr. Platt in New York. She knows Dr. Wheeler."

"She does? Small world."

"Well, knows *of* her. Dr. Wheeler is the foremost authority on sibling grief. It's a somewhat ignored area. When a child dies, people focus on the parents, who are experiencing an unimaginable loss. Less attention goes to the siblings."

"Do you feel that way? Like you're being ignored?"

"No." Sofia watched a bird float on the wind in the distance. "Maybe it's because we're all adults. I feel like I'm in it with my mom and dad. But I…" She sighed and rubbed one thumbnail over the other.

"What?"

"I feel guilty."

"Because you're alive and he's not?"

"It's a little more complicated than that. Anthony never got to do some things he planned to. Things my parents hoped for. Now that he's gone those expectations are on me. Does that make sense?"

"Perhaps. As long as those things don't prevent you from what you want also."

Sofia shrugged. "I'll just have to figure out how to do it all."

Jim turned onto a short drive where Sofia could see the lodge ahead. Two story, with beautiful wood siding, it was much larger than she expected. Pretty stonework became visible around the foundation as they got closer, as well as a stone chimney. An a-frame room at one end had floor-to-ceiling windows and an enormous deck running around the back of the building. The building was surrounded by Aspen trees just starting to turn gold. The location didn't feel isolated, but wonderfully private. This would be an artist's dream spot, let alone a vacation getaway if that's what Jim had in mind for the lodge.

"Wow, this is amazing," she said, getting out of the truck.

"Remember, the outside looks better than the inside."

She leaned into the truck and pulled out her camera bag. "This is exciting."

"It's a ton of work." Jim walked to the door, unlocking and gesturing for her to enter. "You go ahead. I'm going to grab a card table and folding chairs I brought."

The building was dark and cool even though the temperature outside held onto the end of summer heat. Sofia headed toward the windows overlooking the deck, gazing up at the wood ceiling en route.

Gorgeous.

Jim's boots were loud on the floor as he came inside and set up the table and chairs near a window. "I have to get the electricity turned on still. I do have a couple big flashlights in case the upstairs and the basement are dark."

"Your dad may come out to look at your mom's sculptures with us."

"Really? I'm surprised." Jim stood with his hands on his hips. "So, what do you think?"

"It's fantastic. I mean, it needs a lot of work, but

it has so much potential. What's that mattress over there?" Sofia pointed to a corner of the room.

"Yeah, don't go near that. I'm sure it is filled with mice and spiders."

Sofia shook all over and stuck out her tongue. "Yuck."

Jim laughed. "My mom was dedicated to her art. I don't remember her doing this, but dad says she slept here pretty often. She'd get lost in her work and he didn't want her driving winding roads in the dark."

"I wish I could have met your mom."

"Me too. She would have enjoyed you."

Sofia grinned. "That's a nice thing to say."

A knock and a "hello?" turned Jim's attention away from her. "Here we go." He headed to the front and opened the door. "Hey, Larry, glad you could make it. Come in. This is Sofia." He gestured her direction and she waved. "Larry's here to check out the foundation."

For the next three hours, a steady stream of contractors stopped by to take a look at the property inside and out. Sofia chatted with some of the men waiting for Jim. Speaking with the female plumber came easier, and Sofia ended up walking through a lot of the building with her, even going upstairs before Jim had a chance to.

She had just sat down in one of the folding chairs when a familiar voice called hello. "Ben, is that you?"

"I thought you and Jim might be getting hungry. I brought some sandwiches and drinks." He entered the room and set a bag on the table.

"Jim's outside somewhere with someone." Sofia laughed. "I've lost track. It's been non-stop action."

Ben took a seat and opened the bag, pulling out a plastic container with sandwiches inside. "Here. Have a PB&J."

"I'm starving. Thank you."

"That's a good sign. I've noticed you don't eat much."

Sofia smiled and chewed. "Today's been a good day so far. I've felt…useful."

Ben scratched his cheek. "I'm hoping Jim can give Jett something to do too. Jett has the construction experience. He also has a good design eye."

Sofia tilted her head. "What ideas does Jett have for the lodge?"

Ben rocked his head back and forth. "He talks about the lodge as if it doesn't mean anything to him. Granted, he's the youngest and he doesn't remember it as well as Jim and Kai. I think he understands what it could be. By the way the lodge has a pool too. Anyway, Jett's mentioned the idea of adding four to five additional structures to the property. Like cabins or small homes."

"Oh, I like that," Sofia said. "People could have weddings here and stay in the homes. Or family reunions. Or writer retreats."

"Exactly." Ben nodded.

The door closed. "Hi, Dad," Jim called and entered the room. "Saw your truck outside. Food, thank God. I'm hungry." He picked up a sandwich.

"Hey, I went upstairs with the plumber lady and you were right. There are eight rooms up there," Sofia said. "And your dad just told me about a cool idea Jett has for the property. He wants to build additional cabins or little homes for other people to stay in."

"Uh huh." Jim took a bite. "Maybe."

Ben slapped his hands on the table and stood. "That's something you can work out with your brother. I like the idea. Sofia likes it too." Ben winked at her. "I'm here to go down to the basement and look at your mother's sculptures."

"You don't like Jett's idea?" she whispered, walking with Jim and following Ben to the stairs.

"We can talk about it later. Hold on, Dad. Let me go first. I have a flashlight."

Sofia crossed her arms and shivered at the bottom of the basement steps. Walk-out glass doors and a few windows provided enough light to see a room packed with sculptures.

With his hand on the back of a large sculpture of a cow, Ben said, "This was not one of Catherine's favorites. She was working on it when she found out she was pregnant with Jett. I think she felt like she had to keep it, for that reason."

Sofia squeezed between a sculpture of an eagle with its wings spread and one of a four-foot bush, each branch covered with butterflies. "I had no idea they were all this large."

"Most of her sculptures were meant for outdoors." Ben smoothed his hand over a sculpture of a hawk, its talons clutching a rabbit. "She liked the idea that people would touch them."

Across the room, Jim's back was to her and Ben as they moved around the room. "Do you have a favorite, Jim?"

"What?" He turned. "No. I don't know. Not really."

"Here's a small one." Ben walked to her with his hands cupped. "A frog."

"Look at that. You know what I would do? I would incorporate all these into the design of the lodge and the little homes Jett suggested. You could put sculptures on all the paths in-between buildings. Throughout the whole property. People would love that. Wouldn't that be neat?"

"Neat," Jim said with a scowl on his face.

"What do I know?" She waved a hand in the air. "I'm just spit-balling."

Rubbing the back of his neck, Jim walked toward the stairs. "Sorry to cut this whole thing short, but I just remembered I need to meet one of the contractors in town instead. Dad, could you take Sofia with you?"

"Of course," Ben answered, glancing up from his study of a mountain lion climbing down a rock. "I guess I'll have plenty of chances to look at all these again."

Jim's flashlight seemed more like a spotlight on the tension in the air as he led the way, stomping up the stairs.

"Um, Jim, do you and I come back tomorrow and do this all over again?"

"Not tomorrow. I'll let you know about the day after that." He dug his keys out of his pocket without even looking at her. "I'll text you."

Nice.

"Sofia, what do you say we stop at Patsy's Diner on the way home?" Ben asked. "You ate all of two bites of your sandwich. We could get milkshakes."

Okay, so we're all pretending we're not feeling the awkwardness, is that it?

She faced Ben and beamed an overly toothy smile. "I'd love to get a milkshake."

Outside, Ben helped her into the truck and got in himself. "Don't take it personally."

"So I'm not crazy. I did upset him."

"*You* didn't upset him." Ben backed up and headed down the driveway. "He's upset though. Lord, my sons are more alike than different. One bottles up their feelings and the other drinks from it to stay numb."

She pressed her lips together and nodded. "Feelings stink."

Ben's laugh burst out. "They do."

"I think I upset Jim by mentioning Jett's idea."

Ben glanced at her, then back to the road. "It's a good idea, isn't it? Jett's smart. I just wish…he had an anchor. Other than a few teenage antics, Jim's always been the disciplined one. A perfectionist at times. I was hoping the lodge would be a way for them to rely on each other's strengths and cancel out any weaknesses."

"They don't know they're lucky to have each other. Maybe it will just take some time."

"I'm sorry. You don't need me rattling on about this family's struggles."

She leaned back, turning her head toward the window.

Maybe I will call Dr. Wheeler in the morning.

Chapter 9

IT ENDED UP BEING MORE than a couple days before Jim saw Sofia again. He kept her updated by text about needing time to travel north to Four Bears to meet with an architect. It wasn't a lie. That was where he went.

But you did lie. About having a favorite sculpture, when she asked you. Why wasn't it in the basement?

On Friday, Rafe called to tell him he was en route early, and they agreed to meet at a restaurant in the little town around the mountain from Ashnee Valley for dinner.

He stood and shook hands with Rafe when he entered La Pinata around four-thirty. "Hey, man." Jim gestured to a table near a window where they could sit. Rafe took off his baseball cap and rubbed his hand over his long salt and pepper hair. He wore an orange t-shirt with a giant sun on it. Tan, with weathered skin and a beard, he appeared a walking advertisement for the chill life. "You look good, for an old man. How was the drive?"

"Dude, I am old. You wait until you're almost fifty." Rafe turned to the waitress who arrived at the table with chips and asked for their drink orders. "I'll have whatever local beer you have on tap."

"Make that two," Jim added.

"So you're up here talking to an architect?"

"A couple of them. I'm not sure I've found the right one."

"Is your brother still doing construction? He probably knows some good ones."

Jim scooped guacamole on a chip. "I didn't ask him."

"I take it he's still drinking?"

Jim nodded.

Rafe thanked the waitress as she set down his beer. "I'm sorry to hear that. How's everything going with Sofia Russo?"

He ignored Rafe's stupid grin. "Fine. You'll meet her tomorrow. Kai and Leo are hosting a cookout. Dad will be there. I imagine Jett will make an appearance. It will be the first time she meets all the kids."

"Sounds good."

"She's helping with the lodge." Jim paused to take a swallow of beer. "Sort of. She has some interesting ideas. She's a photographer. I have her taking pictures of everything."

"Interesting ideas, like what?"

"Incorporating my mom's sculptures in the design. Not just in the building but some pathways around the property too." He picked at the label on his bottle, peeling the corner back.

"That's creative. She sounds smart."

"Creative. Smart. Sexy."

"Now I get what's got you all twisted up." Rafe leaned back in his chair. "You don't seem that thrilled about her idea."

"It's a good idea. I didn't expect all this to be as hard as it already is."

"Ah." Rafe nodded. "She's an added distraction you didn't want, is that it?"

Jim held his hand up. "Don't start with your analysis. She's good looking. Okay. Maybe, gorgeous."

"Maybe?" Rafe laughed. "One, I was there at the robbery. Two, I have access to the Internet in New Mexico. I've seen her photo. What's the problem?"

"I like her. I feel good when I'm around her. But, whatever, she's going back to New York sometime soon. Otherwise, I feel shitty around Jett. I worry about my dad."

"It's not easy to come home. You just got here. There's a lot of family emotions around the lodge. Hell, I remember sleeping there right after your mom died. I've never been around a man as destroyed as your dad. I felt guilty he was paying me."

"I don't remember you sleeping there."

Rafe laughed. "I was so fucking broke. I was on leave from the Army. I don't think your dad cared. He hired me to close up the place before winter and asked me to move the sculptures to the basement."

"Dad didn't care about anything after Mom

died. For years. Why'd he do that anyway?"

"Put everything in the basement? I think he thought he was going to show the place and sell it, but then could never bring himself to do it."

Jim ordered tacos and Rafe a burrito when the waitress stopped at the table. "Has your dad forgiven me for talking you into joining the military?"

"It's Kai that hasn't forgiven you. Now that I'm home for good, she might say hello."

"We made a good team. Protected a lot of Marines and Seals in our day. I'm glad to be done with it though. And I'm glad you asked me to come up to work on the lodge. I'm still thinking about our conversation earlier, about investing in it. I like the idea of us being partners again. Who knows, maybe I'll relocate up here for good. There's more than one reason to stay in the area."

Jim grimaced. "Are you still fantasizing you could get Doc Cindy to give you the time of day?"

Rafe scratched the top of his head. "Talk about a distraction. That woman does it for me."

"You've only seen a photo of her. You're like a beast to her beauty."

"Yeah, well. First things first. I'm looking forward to seeing the family and formally meeting Sofia."

Twenty-four hours later, Jim pulled out of his driveway with Rafe in the passenger seat of his truck and headed to Kai's house. He parked next to Jett's vehicle and glanced in the rearview mirror as his father followed up the driveway with Sofia.

Rafe rubbed his hands together and got out of the truck.

"Jesus, it begins," Jim mumbled and slammed his door. Rafe put his hands on the roof of his dad's vehicle, leaning to look in the window. "Mr. Mannis, good to see you, sir. And this must be the one and only Sofia. I'm Rafe."

Her smile was tentative as she came around the car and shook Rafe's hand. "Hi." Turning she gave him a tiny wave. "Hey, Jim."

"Hey," he answered, wanting suddenly to kick his own ass for ignoring her the last few days. Her white short-sleeve sweater, brown skirt, and tan legs drew his eye.

"Smooth talker," Rafe whispered as he passed by, heading into the house with Ben, leaving Sofia alone with him in the driveway.

"How've you been the last few days?" he asked.

"Good. I hope your meetings went well. Did you find an architect to work with?"

"Not yet." He squeezed the back of his neck. "Listen, I'm sorry about the other day. At the lodge. I was rude. Cutting you and Dad off early."

She shrugged her shoulder. "I shouldn't have suggested anything about the designs for the lodge. It isn't my place. Your mom was a great artist. I got excited."

She stared at the gravel in the driveway, tapping a stone with her foot.

I'm an idiot.

Stepping close he put a hand on her upper arm. "I don't want you to feel that way. Your idea about the sculptures is a good one. I want you to feel like you can talk to me, okay? About the lodge or anything."

"I did decide I need to speak to someone here about Anthony's death. I made an appointment with Dr. Wheeler for tomorrow."

He squeezed her arm. "I'm glad." She still wasn't making eye contact and he couldn't take it. "Hey." He let go her arm and put a finger beneath her chin, gently. "Are you okay?" His heart lurched when she shook her head. "If this cookout is too much, we don't have to stay. We can go."

"Some days are better than others. I'm a little nervous."

"Let's have a signal. You can let me know that way. We can go. Anytime. I can take you back to Dad's."

Or my house.

"Okay." She bit her lip. "I'll tug on my ear, how's that?"

"Perfect," Jim said. "And if I grab my own neck and choke myself out, that's how you'll know I want to leave." To his relief, she cracked up at his silly joke.

"Hello, you two." Kai called from the door. "Are you coming in? The kids are anxious to meet Sofia."

Jim put his hand on the small of her back directing her through his sister's house and toward the deck where the family gathered. The smell of hamburgers and hotdogs cooking on the grill greeted him as they stepped through the sliding glass door. Leo introduced Sofia to each of his kids along with some of the kids' friends who were visiting too. After a flurry of 'nice to meet you,' he chuckled as all the kids ran off into the yard. Only four-year old Suze remained with the adults, her arms wrapped around one of her mother's legs. Leo joined the kids in the yard and Ben sat on the deck.

Jim took over grilling and Rafe gestured for Sofia to sit in the chair next to him. "How are you doing since the robbery?"

"Rafe was there." Jim flipped a couple burgers. "He saw you first, before I did."

"Correction, I saw the guy with the gun first."

"Right," Jim answered with a quick glance to Sofia, who had a hand on her chest, blinking rapidly.

"*Then* I saw her in the white dress before you took him out."

Jim flinched as his sister plopped Suze in Rafe's lap, quickly pulled Sofia from her chair and walked her into the house, an arm around her shoulders.

"What the...is she crying?" Jim asked. Seeing her mom escort the weeping Sofia away, Suze had begun to sob.

"Shit, I'm sorry." Rafe held the four-year-old away from his body in mid-air. "I guess we startled her."

"We?" Jim picked up his niece, hugging her against his chest. "Have you never held a kid before? Jesus."

"What's the matter, pumpkin?" Leo called from the edge of the deck. "Is Uncle Jim scaring you?"

"I didn't scare anyone. Dipshit here made Sofia cry and then Suze started crying too."

Ben whistled loudly. "Do you think you could stop swearing? You're worse than the teenagers in the yard. Bring Suze here, then go in the house and talk with Sofia."

"Yes, sir." Jim shot daggers at Rafe who opened his hands and mouthed "what?" After handing off his niece, he went inside and found the two women sitting at the kitchen table.

"Kai, would you excuse us for a second." He put his hand out to Sofia then led her through the house and out the front door. On the porch, he pulled her into his arms and held her. "Fuck, I'm sorry. We didn't mean to spring anything on you. We're just dumb idiots, especially Rafe." Over her head, he saw Jett backing out at the end of the driveway.

She tapped her cast against his back. Her voice was muffled against his shirt, but her body shook with a tiny laugh. "Stop." She squeezed her arms tighter. "Can we just stay like this a minute?"

We can stay like this all night.

"Of course."

Eventually, she stepped out of his arms and wiped under her eyes. "Would you point me to the nearest bathroom and then grab my purse from the kitchen table please?"

"How is she?" His father asked when he came

out on the deck.

"She's okay now." He opened the top of the cooler and grabbed a beer. "Where'd Jett go, by the way? I didn't even see him."

"Who knows." Kai answered. "He was here in the yard for a few minutes, said hi to the kids and left."

Good. There's one saving grace.

"Okay, let's get everyone to the table." Kai smiled past him. "Here she is." She linked arms with Sofia. "You and Rafe are down there." Kai pointed him to the other end of the table. "Dad, come sit next to Sofia and me."

He gave his sister a sour look and sat next to his nephew, Will, and across from his niece, Jocelyn, and her friend, Nicki, who stuck their heads together, giggling.

After dinner he sat on the deck with his dad and Leo, watching the sunset. Relieved that no one cried during the meal, he enjoyed soft voices and occasional laughs coming through the kitchen window where Kai, Suze, and Sofia were hanging out.

Impressive. I would have tugged on my ear hours ago.

"I'm heading home now." Ben stood and put a hand on Leo's shoulder. "Thank you. This was nice. Tell the kids I'll see them in a few days." He turned Jim's direction. "I'll leave the backdoor unlocked."

"Thanks, Dad. I'll drop Sofia off in a little bit."

"I like her," Leo said when they were alone

again.

Jim smiled. "She's easy to like." He put down his cup. "I'm going to check if she's ready to leave. It's starting to get dark. Rafe should be back soon from taking the kids fishing."

It was quiet when he entered the house and passed through the empty kitchen. He followed the low murmur of voices down the hall toward the bedrooms. Peeking into the girls' room he saw Sofia sitting on the floor, her back against the side of Suze's bed. Only Kai's legs hanging over the edge of Jocelyn's bed were visible from where he stood. His sister's voice soothing as she read a bedtime story. From her perch on the bed Suze haphazardly put multi-colored barrettes in Sofia's hair.

He opened the door further and stuck his head in. "It's nice and peaceful in here. Great job, Suze. She looks like a million bucks." His niece bounced on the bed. "Dad left," he said to Kai and then turned to Sofia. "Ready to take off when Rafe gets back?"

She nodded, then let her head fall back on the bed and made a silly upside-down face at Suze. "Time for my beauty sleep."

"Booty sweep," Suze repeated and put her arms wide. Jim crossed the room to gather a hug. "Love you, Suze Q. I'll come back in a few minutes."

On the ride home, Sofia sat wedged between him and Rafe in the truck. He was all too aware of her body pressed against his side.

"I'm tired." She leaned her head against his shoulder for a second, then lifted it nearly as fast as if she suddenly remembered where she was.

"What time is your appointment tomorrow?"

"I see Dr. Wheeler at ten or ten-thirty. I don't remember at the moment. I didn't bring my phone. It's on there, though."

"How are you getting downtown? Do you need a ride?"

"Doc Wheeler? I can take her," Rafe chimed in. "What's your phone number? You can text me the time and I'll pick you up in the morning."

Jim glanced past Sofia. "Are you serious?"

"Serious as a heart attack." Rafe smiled at Sofia. "We got off to a bad start earlier when I scared you by bringing up the robbery. I'd like to make up for it."

"That's not why you're offering to give her a ride. Tell her the real reason."

There was little room to move in the truck but Rafe turned enough to face Sofia. "I am completely and utterly twitter-pated with Doc Wheeler."

"I get it. I'm a little intimidated by all the credentials."

"I know, right?" Rafe put his head back and closed his eyes. "Did you see the photo of her in the rose-colored pantsuit?"

"Yes!" Sofia's voice rose with excitement. "On the website? With the matching everything. Shirt, pants, jacket and shoes. Who even has a full body shot with their bio? I guess people who are that amazing."

"I could die a happy man if she'd just give me a chance."

"That'll be the day," Jim said.

"Don't listen to him, Rafe." Sofia nudged her elbow into his side as he pulled up to the house and put the truck in park. "Of course you can give me a ride."

Chapter 10

IN THE MORNING, SOFIA CLIMBED the stairs to Dr. Wheeler's office above the Queen Bee Bookstore in downtown Ashnee Valley. She'd left Rafe on the street below. He offered to meet her in the lobby of Dr. Wheeler's office in an hour, and she smiled knowingly, wiggling he eyebrows. "Sounds good."

Entering, she found an empty reception desk and two closed doors. Soft voices carried from one of the rooms. She was a few minutes early, so she sat on a comfortable white couch next to a small round table. Muted recessed lighting gave the room a soft glow. The walls and carpet were a soft gray. Other than her chair, the room was monochrome. It reminded her of Rafe's fascination with Dr. Wheeler's rose-colored outfit.

She sat up straight when an office door opened, then stood as Dr. Cindy Wheeler walked toward her smiling. "Sofia? Hi." She put a hand out to shake. "Come on back."

The room was warm with a colorful oriental

rug and brown leather furniture and several plants. Unlike her professional photo, Dr. Wheeler wore different colors – black bootleg cut slacks, a white V-neck sweater, and black pumps. Perfect pearl earrings adorned her ears. Half glasses hung from a silver chain like a necklace.

"Should I sit on the couch?" Sofia asked.

"Couch or chair, wherever you like is fine." Dr. Wheeler opened a mini-fridge. "Would you like a water?"

"Thank you." She held up her cast. "You'll have to open it for me, if you don't mind."

"I don't mind at all. When does the cast come off?"

"I think in a couple weeks. I broke it recently." Sofia sat in a brown leather chair and Dr. Wheeler took a seat in a similar chair across from her.

"I spoke with Dr. Platt. She called with your referral. She mentioned you've been seeing her since sometime in June."

"Yes." Sofia bit her lip. "My brother died in early June."

"That's such a short time ago. I'm so sorry. What brought about the decision to visit Colorado?"

"Dr. Platt didn't mention why?"

"No." Dr. Wheeler tilted her head. "Just a quick referral, one doctor to another."

"I was part of a bank robbery. Wait, that sounds wrong." She laughed nervously glancing up. "I was caught in the middle of a bank robbery. The security guard was shot. I helped him and he lived. Jim Mannis was the police officer that saved my life. He shot the gunman, who later died."

"This was how long ago?"

"About two weeks. There was a lot of media attention on it. On me. Some crazy people were threatening online to kill me. Someone smashed my apartment window with a brick. It seemed a good idea to get away from New York for a bit. Let things settle down. Jim was already coming back here and got stuck bringing me with him."

Dr. Wheeler smiled when she made eye contact. "That must have been very frightening. I didn't mean to make you jump in so fast. Is this the first time you've talked about the robbery since you got here?"

"Yes. I mostly wanted to see you about my brother. Everyone thinks it would be a good idea to keep talking to someone."

"Who's everyone?"

"Well, my parents, my best friend, Dr. Platt, and the entire Mannis family."

"And you?"

Sofia shrugged. "I suppose."

Dr. Wheeler got up and walked to a small desk and picked up a leather notebook. "Are you okay if I write some things down while we talk?"

"Sure."

"I've known the Mannis family off and on my whole life. You probably know that?"

"Yes. I know you lost a sister."

Dr. Wheeler nodded. "I did. Cammie. She was my twin and she drowned in a flood when we were five years old."

"I'm sorry, Dr. Wheeler."

"Me too. You can call me Cindy."

"Jim calls you Doc Cindy." Sofia smiled.

"A lot of people in Ashnee Valley do. The Mannises are a good family. They know their share of grief too. Most families do, but that doesn't make this any easier, does it?"

"No," she choked out. "I didn't want to cry." Sofia took a tissue from the box Cindy held out. "I want to put myself back together, my life, and go home."

"That's understandable. What was your life like in New York?"

Sofia held the tissue tight in her hand as she stared out the small office window. "Before Anthony got sick and died, it was perfect. I had my photography career, my best friend, my parents. Anthony lived nearby."

"Anthony was older or younger?"

"Four years younger. I'm twenty-nine and he had just turned twenty-five before he passed away."

"One thing that can help when someone dies is working through how to reconcile a prior life with a new life."

Sofia closed her eyes. "That sounds a little like Dr. Platt wanting me to unpack the past."

"It doesn't sound like that's what you're looking for. So, what do you mean when you say, 'put yourself together?'"

Sofia sighed. "It means, getting back to New York. Getting my old job back. Moving closer to my parents. Finding a husband. Having kids."

"And that was the plan before your brother died?"

"No," Sofia blurted, heat spreading across her cheeks.

"Go on."

"That wasn't the plan." Her frustration rose along with her voice. "I saw myself in New York. I saw myself as a photographer."

"What about the other things on the list?"

Marriage? Maybe.

Moving back to Staten Island? Never.

Kids? No, but I'll do it for Anthony. For my parents.

The sound of a door closing outside the room made her look to the clock on the wall. "That's probably my ride." Sofia sucked in a breath and puffed it out. "Can we stop for today?"

"Of course," Cindy said. "If you'd like to come back, I have appointments on Tuesdays and Fridays. I'm working on a book the rest of the time. You could come once a week or twice a week or play it by ear."

Sofia scooted to the edge of her seat. "I'd like to come back on Tuesday."

"Good, let's meet at the same time then." Cindy handed her a business card and stood. "My personal cell number is on the back. Don't hesitate to call for any reason. Come on, I'll walk you out."

She expected Rafe to be in the lobby when she walked out of the doctor's office. Instead, Jim sat on the couch.

"Hi, Doc." He stood and stuck out his hand. "It's been a long time."

Affection emanated off Cindy as she gently swatted Jim's hand and hugged him instead.

"Jim. It's been forever. I understand you are home for good this time. Your family must be thrilled about that."

"For the most part. Jett and I are still working things through." Jim turned Sofia's direction. "How'd it go?"

"Good. I'm going to meet with Dr. Wheeler again next Tuesday." Sofia fiddled with the strap of her purse, trying not to appear too engaged in their reunion.

"Cindy," Dr. Wheeler reminded her before facing Jim again. "I've seen Jett since I got back to Ashnee Valley."

Jim's eyebrows shot up. "You have?"

"Around town mostly."

Sofia absorbed the smallest eyelid twitch on Cindy's face. *I wonder if Jett is her patient too?*

"How's your mom doing? Is she still in Utah?"

"She's fine. My brothers are there too."

"But you couldn't stay away from the thriving metropolis of Ashnee Valley?" Jim grinned.

"Sort of. I'm writing my second book. I took a sabbatical from my practice. I have a few patients here that I see."

"I'm fortunate you can fit me in." Sofia smiled at Cindy then Jim. "I thought Rafe would be here to give me a ride. Not that I'm unhappy to see you."

"I wanted to take you to lunch." Jim turned to Cindy again. "It's great to see you. Tell your mom and brothers I said hello."

"I will. Sofia, I look forward to seeing you again in a few days."

"Thank you."

She followed Jim down the steps to the street from Dr. Wheeler's office. "I'm shocked you got Rafe to give up his spot."

"Yeah, he's ticked off. But there's something I need to talk to you about, just you and me. Are you hungry?"

She put her hand on his arm and stopped walking. "Not now that you said that."

"It's nothing bad." He smiled. "Lieutenant Kincaid called with an update on the robbery suspects. Plus, it's an excuse to have lunch with you."

"You don't need an excuse. You're my only friend. Besides your dad."

Jim tucked her arm in his and began walking again. "Do you miss home?"

"Yes. I miss my mom and dad and Delia."

"Maybe a hamburger and stinky fries would help." Jim gestured to several outdoor tables with red umbrellas. "Indoors or outdoors?"

"Outdoors. What are stinky fries?"

"They're waffle fries with blue cheese on them. You dip them in ranch."

"Sounds like we'll have the windows open on the ride home."

She smiled shyly when Jim cracked up. "I'm a lucky man bringing someone with a sense of humor home with me."

After the waitress brought them each a soda and they placed their orders, Sofia asked about the phone call from New York.

"The good news is that all the suspects from the bank robbery have been arrested. There were more robberies than originally thought. Five altogether in varying parts of New York and New Jersey over the last few months. Lieutenant Kincaid thinks at some point you'll be called to testify. D.A. Nader is getting a lot of accolades. She's pleased."

Sofia took a sip of her drink and wiped condensation from the side of her glass with a finger. "I've never been in a courtroom."

"Maybe they'll gather your deposition by videotape. I wouldn't get too worried about that part at the moment."

She glanced at Jim. "What part would you worry about?"

Jim smiled. "There's nothing to worry about. You're here and everything is fine. However, bringing in all the suspects has ramped up the threats again, that's all. I know you're homesick, but everyone agrees that you should stay here for now. Keep a low profile."

"Oh, everyone agrees? So there's been another discussion among all the macho guys plus my mother?" She put her hand on her chest, "And my part is to smile pleasantly, right?"

He put his hands up. "Macho guys? Slow down a little. It's not like that."

Sofia used the brief pause in conversation when the waitress delivered their burgers and fries to try to calm her rapid pulse.

"By your reaction, I'm guessing you didn't

really want to stay and help with the lodge. I get it. You want to leave. You can't now. And it sucks."

"Really? You're going to act like *you're* hurt because *I'm* not thrilled to have no control over my own life. Who knows how long I'll be stuck here? I'm totally out of the loop in my career. Plus surrounded by men all the time. Why are there no women in this town besides your sister, by the way? Oh wait, now I have Doc Cindy to talk to. Thank God for that." She plunked a waffle fry in dip and smashed it into her mouth. *That's good.* She shook the ketchup bottle, watching as Jim sat back clasping his hands behind his head.

"You've been holding out."

"What are you talking about?" She lifted the top bun and poured ketchup on her burger.

"You're pissed off."

She picked her burger up one-handed, took a bite and spoke around it. "Gee, you think?"

"It's about time."

"I'm glad you approve. I'm sick of being sad. I thought I'd try something new today." She stuffed a fry in her mouth. "Like bitchy."

"It's brought out your appetite." He reached across with his napkin and wiped her cheek. "Kind of sloppy though."

How can he make me want to laugh when I also want to strangle someone?

"It's because I can only use one hand."

"I know. I'll stop teasing you. It's good to see you eat and let a little bit out."

"We can't all be as disciplined as you." She raised her eyebrows at his wide-eyed look. "You're so perfectly behaved."

"What are you trying to say?" He took a bite of his burger then sat back.

"Nothing." She wiped her hands on her napkin. "Forget it. That was not okay of me to say. I'm all over the place emotionally. Stuff came up at my session with Dr. Wheeler. I'm bound to pick a fight with anyone today if I open my mouth."

"You think I'm perfectly behaved?"

"Jim, you are all the right things." She waved her hand. "You have done nothing but be helpful. It's just…"

"Are you trying to tell me I'm boring? What?"

She lifted both shoulders and squirmed in her chair.

Don't say it. Don't say it. Don't say it.

"I'm lonely."

He lowered his chin.

"I don't know, maybe we…"

He blew out a breath. "It's probably better if we stick to boring."

Her cheeks burned as she stared at her lap.

"I can tell what you're thinking. I didn't say that because I wouldn't want to be the man to take your lonely away."

With tears threatening to spill, she shut her eyes.

"Believe me, I wish I was that guy, but it would never be more than temporary. And you're vulnerable right now. You said yourself, today's been tough. I'd never take advantage of that or you. If that makes me perfectly behaved or boring…"

Shaking her head, she picked at her food, then

pushed the plate away. "I never said you were boring."

You know where lonely got you last time. A cringe-worthy night with your boss. Be glad he's not like Robert.

"I have to go back up to Four Bears with Rafe and my dad tomorrow. But how about you and I spend Sunday together and do something fun?"

Sofia swallowed her embarrassment plastering on a fake smile. "Okay, what'd you have in mind?"

"Horseback riding. I'll come by the ranch and we can take some lunch along. We'll hang out outdoors for the day."

"I've never ridden a horse. Can a person even ride a horse with a cast?" She shrugged as if to say the idea was ludicrous. "Seriously?" She added in the hope of getting out of it.

"Sure, you can."

Super!

"Worst case scenario we ride together first time out."

"First time?" She raised her eyebrows. "You're an optimist."

"You bet."

Chapter 11

THE SUN SET LOW IN the sky, just about to slip behind the foothills as Jim enjoyed a beer on his patio at the end of the day.

"Hi." Rafe took a seat near him. "Great view. The only one better is from the deck at the lodge."

"Not bad from the ranch either."

"True. How did your conversation with Sofia go about the news from New York? It better be good since you prevented me from meeting the lovely doctor today."

Jim laughed. "She looks good. I mean, I think of her like a cousin or an aunt. I've known her forever." He hesitated, picking at his beer label before answering the question. "Lunch with Sofia went all right."

Rafe popped the top of his beer and took a swallow. "Just all right?"

He leaned his head back, closed his eyes and groaned. "She told me she's lonely."

"Well, that's normal, I imagine."

"There was more to it than that. She said it with, you know, a look."

"Ah." Rafe took another sip. "The plot thickens. So what'd you say?"

He got out of his chair and paced. "I suggested it would probably be better if we stuck to boring."

Rafe threw his head back laughing and clapped his hands. "What the fuck? Stick to boring, what does that mean?"

He crossed his arms over his chest. "It means I'm not going to take advantage of her. I'm supposed to protect her. I'm a grown up, not some horndog that just wants to get in her pants."

"Okay, okay, simmer down." Rafe held his hands up. "I get the not wanting to take advantage of the situation because she's grieving or whatever. So you go slow, you didn't need to shut her down completely."

Shit.

"You should have seen the look she gave me." He glanced at Rafe, sitting on the edge of his seat grinning.

"Before or after you said the stupid shit?"

"Before." He sat again, running a finger back and forth on his eyebrow. "It's better now than later." He finished his beer, putting the bottle on the table nearby.

"What's that mean? You're home now. It's not like you're still in the service and have to leave anybody. It's okay to settle down. Find a good woman. You obviously like her." Rafe sat back in his chair. "What I'd give for that chance to meet someone…and I'm a lot older than you."

"I can't have kids." Jim clasped his hands behind his head staring straight ahead.

"Really? I didn't know."

Jim sighed. "Nobody does besides my dad. My mom knew."

Rafe scratched his cheek. "You've known for a long time."

"They found it early when I had a groin injury in high school from football. Not all the inner plumbing works. It wasn't the injury. It's got a name. Doesn't matter. I don't want to talk about it anymore." He got up and walked to the patio door and turned back. "I'm going to stick a frozen pizza in the oven. You want another beer?"

"Yes." Rafe jiggled his empty bottle in the air. "Jim, don't you think you're getting ahead of yourself? Not every woman wants kids, and there isn't only one way if she does."

"This one does. She's already decided she's her parents' last chance for a grandchild now that her brother is gone."

Rafe winced. "Oh, boy. I'm sorry. Where'd you leave things with her?"

"We're going to go horseback riding on Sunday."

"Are you trying to make it so she doesn't even want to be friends?"

He pulled his chin back. "What do you mean?"

"She's a city girl. Ease into it. Take her fishing. Have a picnic. Don't toss her up on a thousand-pound animal." Rafe pushed to stand and straightened the legs of his jeans. "I have no idea how you'd survive without me here to help you."

"Thanks, man."

The next morning Rafe headed out first to Four Bears to talk with a couple different construction companies being considered for work on the lodge. Jim leaned his hip against the kitchen counter, eating a bowl of cereal, waiting for his dad to pick him up. The old man insisted on driving which left him feeling less in control than he liked. His thoughts turned to Sofia.

I wonder if she's still sleeping? What's she going to do alone at Dad's house all day? I hope we get back before dinner.

The sound of truck tires on gravel shook him out of his reverie. He put his bowl in the sink and headed out the door.

"Hi, Dad."

"Good morning. I brought an extra thermos with coffee if you want some."

"Thanks. How's Sofia today?"

"Still in her pajamas and robe. She said she was going to try to relax. I guess you're going horseback riding with her tomorrow? I'm not sure she's excited about it."

"I changed my mind. I'm taking her fishing instead."

"You should text her, so she isn't worried all day."

"It's not that big a deal. Everyone is acting like I told her we were going to zip line over a volcano."

"I didn't say that. Who said that?"

"Rafe gave me the same advice. Whatever. I stayed up late and drank too many beers last night." He opened the thermos and blew as a cloud of steam escaped. "Forget it. Sorry I snapped at you."

"Well, I suspect you won't like what I have to say next either."

He put his head back and closed his eyes.

"I'm not feeling certain about how things are progressing with the lodge," Ben continued.

Jim dropped his shoulders. "What do you mean? I've been meeting with contractors left and right. Rafe's up in Four Bears already talking to a couple construction companies. We're on our way to meet with two architects. What is not going the way you want?"

When his father glanced away from the road looking over the top of his glasses at him, he sucked in a breath, held it and let it out. "I can't go any faster, Dad."

"It's not about speed. I'm concerned because your brother and sister aren't involved."

He put his hands out. "Kai doesn't have time. I already talked to her and Leo about that." He tried to lower his voice but failed. "Just say it. Who we're really talking about is Jett. What do you want me to do, put an alcoholic in charge?"

"Cool it." His father answered in a low voice.

He pushed back against his seat, tapping his chest. "I'm not the one that needs to cool it."

"Like it or not, I'm the one funding this restoration. So, yes, you do. It's supposed to bring all of you kids together."

"Well you should have thought of that sentiment a long time ago. Like after Mom died and you checked out on everyone. Maybe that's why Kai got pregnant so young. Why I joined the Army and why Jett drinks. I'm not his father, you are."

Ben pulled the truck to the side of the road with a jerky motion, slapping the steering wheel with his hand. "This is about your mother's legacy. Don't you think I know I let you kids down after she died? I have to live with that the rest of my life. Knowing none of you may ever forgive me. Knowing you left because I pressured you. Because of me."

The hurt on his dad's face stung worse than a slap. Jim lowered his head. "I'm sorry. I had no right to speak to you like that. I woke up in a foul mood. That's no excuse."

He rubbed a finger over his chin as his father pulled the truck back onto the road without another word. Glancing at his father's stern profile, he groaned inwardly. "I don't know how to approach Jett or how to work with him. We're barely speaking. How can I rely on him?"

"I know, son." Ben shook his head. "You know there was a time when you two had fun together. I thought the lodge would be a way Jett could find himself again. You're the natural born leader in this family, but he's smart and he has construction experience. If he could build his confidence, maybe he can quit drinking." He lifted his hand from the steering wheel in a fist. "Before I die, I want that boy to get himself together."

"Yeah, me too." Jim answered. "Let's just get through today first. Hopefully, we'll find an architect and a construction company to hire. Then I'll figure out a way to bring Jett in. No more talk about you dying, either."

His father nodded. "Okay."

Jim burned his tongue on a sip of coffee. *This is going to be a long day.*

Sofia wrapped her cast in plastic for the umpteenth time and took a long shower. August had transitioned to September and the temperatures were slightly lower. She wore jeans instead of shorts and a white t-shirt with a lightweight pink cardigan. The sun streaked across the kitchen table. The tick-tock of an old-fashioned clock on the windowsill over the sink reminded her of her grandparents' house. Stretching, she raised her arms over her head. Her heart picked up speed at the sound of a vehicle. She got up to look out the window.

Jett. What is he doing here?

With a hand to her chest, she searched the kitchen as if something there would quell her nerves. Flinching at his knock, she took a deep breath and opened the door.

"Hi. What brings you by?"

"What brings me by?" Jett mimicked her formality in a sing-song manner. "I stopped to ask Dad if he wanted to get some breakfast. His truck is gone so I take it he went over to the senior center or something."

"No, actually. He and Jim are on their way to Four Bears for some appointments."

Jett cocked his head to the side. "They left you here all alone?"

Sofia walked backward, then picked up her coffee mug from the table carrying it to the counter to refill it. "Yup. Do you want some coffee? I could probably make you some eggs if you want."

"You don't have to do that, but thanks for the offer. I'll have some coffee." Jett opened the fridge. "I'll make myself some toast if that's okay with you?"

"Of course." She put his drink on the table and sat again, watching as he put bread in the toaster.

"What are you up to today?" he asked.

"Um, nothing really. Maybe I'll take a walk later. It's such a pretty day."

"Do you want to go fishing? I have all my gear in my truck."

"I don't know if I should go far." She rubbed her temple. "I'm not sure when everyone will get back."

"There's a small lake on the ranch. We could walk there." His back was to her as he spread butter and jam on his toast. "Have you ever been fishing?" he asked as he walked to the table.

"Me? No."

"A lot of people go fly-fishing around here, but I don't think that'd be a good start for you. Open-reel is simpler and it's just a pond, not even a lake really and definitely not a river. We probably won't catch anything."

Sofia smiled. "First of all, open-reel means nothing to me versus fly-fishing. Second, why go if you won't catch anything?"

"People fish for all sorts of reasons. There are actually fishing competition shows on TV. For others it's dinner." He shrugged. "I find it relaxing and an excuse to sit in the sunshine. It's fun. I can teach you how to bait a hook and cast. Like I said, it's unlikely we'll catch anything, but if you do, I can help you reel it in since you can't use both hands."

She ran her index finger around the rim of her mug.

"Do you need to call Jim and ask his permission first?"

Sofia pursed her lips at his smirk. "Very funny and no, I don't. Okay, yes. Let's go fishing."

"Awesome. I'll finish up and we can head out."

She put the coffee mugs in the dishwasher then glanced out the kitchen window at Jett, pulling rods and a tackle box from the back of his truck. He picked up a net then threw it back again. Debating whether to bring her camera, she ultimately voted against the idea. Once outside, she walked across the driveway toward Jett. "Should I lock the door?"

"Nah." He shook his head. "It won't matter. Here."

Sofia took the rod he handed her. "How do I carry this? Like a Continental soldier?" She put the rod against her shoulder and used her cast to salute.

Jett grabbed a bucket from the truck bed.

"That's as good a way as any."

"I can carry something else if you want." She said as they started walking around the back of the house through the grass.

"I got it." Jett used the fishing rod in his hand like a pointer. "We're headed that direction. See that line of trees? The pond is just past that."

"It's closer than I thought. Do you fish here often?"

"No. I don't come by the ranch too much."

"It's amazing here. I didn't know what I was missing in New York. It is something to look at Mercy Mountain each day. It gives me confidence that not everything changes." She laughed at herself, stepping a little higher as taller grass brushed against her pantlegs.

"I get what you mean. We all need something solid to rely on. Nature never lets me down."

"It's like an anchor for you, then?"

She pulled up short when he stopped walking and turned back. "Starting the fishing a little early, aren't you?"

"Was it that obvious?"

"Uh, yeah." Jett raised his voice imitating her. "So, gee whiz Jett, nature's like an anchor and yet here you are the black sheep of the family, what's that about?"

Sofia laughed. "That's a pretty big leap you're making." She shrugged. "Okay, yeah, I'm fishing a bit trying to figure you out."

"What do you want to know, baby girl?"

She rested the end of the rod on the ground, holding it like a spear. "Don't do that."

"Ask me whatever you want to know…Sofia."

She followed him now single file as the path narrowed leading toward the trees. "The other day," she began, "your dad was telling me an idea you brought up for the lodge and the property around it. He liked it. He said you have a lot of construction experience. I was wondering if you had other ideas too?"

"You mean building little houses in addition to renovating the lodge?"

"Yeah. It's a great idea." She picked up her pace behind him so she could hear better as he spoke over his shoulder.

"I figured the houses could be rented out separately or together. It would expand what we could offer. And the Little Forest Fairgrounds butts up against our property. There are lots of events held there. We could dovetail with those too."

"Maybe there could be paths in between buildings and your mother's sculptures could be incorporated with little signs about them or about her or something."

"That's clever. I like that. My mom kept sketch books and a diary about her art. I'll try to find some of that stuff. It's either in the lodge or Jim's house. The other idea I had was naming the cabins." He stopped talking as they reached the water and put down his gear. "I didn't really think this through, like bringing something for us to sit on."

"I don't mind getting a little dirty. Should we sit here?"

"Yeah. We'll bait our hooks and then I'll show you how to cast."

She plopped herself on the ground, looking up. "What were you going to say about naming the cabins?"

He sat next to her and took an old coffee can out of the bucket he carried. "It's a little corny. You know how places name rooms, like, after all the rivers in an area or after the states?"

She nodded, looking at the dirt inside the coffee can when Jett took the plastic lid off.

"My idea is to name the rooms and cabins after family members. Mainly Kai's kids so they feel included. So, Suze's Cabin. Jocelyn's Cabin. And so on. The main hall in the lodge would be named after my mom. Catherine Hall. That one was actually Jim's idea." He dug his fingers into the dirt and held a wiggling object in front of her. "Here's your bait." Picking up her hand, he dropped the worm in the middle of her palm.

"Oh, cool."

"Cool?" He chuckled. "I was waiting for you to scream."

"Why would I scream? By the way, I love the naming idea." She smiled. "I want to see your dad's face when he hears about Catherine Hall. I think he'll love it."

Jett pulled another worm from the can. "Watch and learn." He threaded the bait to the hook. "Think you can handle that or would you rather I do it?"

Sofia picked up the worm with the tips of her fingers on her cast side then used her other hand to wrap the bait on the hook.

"Good job." Jett stood, putting out his hand to

pull her up. "I don't know if my ideas will get past the gate-keeper. We aren't exactly talking."

"Jim."

"Yep." Jett headed toward the edge of the pond and she followed. "Okay, just watch me a few times and then we'll get you started."

For the next several minutes she listened to Jett's instructions, loving the whiz of the line when he cast over the water. He stood far from her when she tried, her line making it a few feet the first several times before he demonstrated how to relax and let the line flow as if an extension from her arm. She sat cross-legged next to him once both lines were in the water.

"Do what I'm doing," he said. "I tug a little on the line every so often and reel it in slowly."

She wiggled her shoulders. "Look at me. I'm fishing."

He glanced her way. "You're a natural, Sis."

She couldn't prevent the tear from falling down her cheek at his choice of words.

"Hey." He took the rod out of her hand. "Are you crying? Is it because I called you sis?"

She inhaled and wiped her cheek with her sleeve. "It's okay. It just hits me like a wave sometimes that my brother is really gone. It stinks when it shows up out of the blue and makes everyone uncomfortable."

"It doesn't make me uncomfortable. I get it. I am sorry though. I'd never try to make you sad."

"I know you wouldn't." She swallowed. "Today's been nice. Thank you for taking me fishing."

Jett rocked his head side to side with a small

smile. "I have my moments. I'm working on stringing a few of my good ones together. Thanks for coming with me."

Chapter 12

JIM'S HEAD THROBBED AS HE drove toward the ranch house, his eyes fixated on Jett's truck parked in front. "What the hell is he doing here?"

"Try not to jump to any conclusions," Ben said. They parked and got out. "He stops by occasionally."

"On the one day you or I'm not here, but Sofia is?" Jim slammed his door and walked around the truck. "Just great." He gestured to the fishing rods leaning against the house by the back door.

"Looks like someone beat you to taking Sofia fishing."

"Thanks, Dad. I appreciate you pointing out the obvious," Jim muttered. "Worst goddamn day ever." He headed up the steps, opened the door, and followed his father inside.

"Hi," Sofia said from the kitchen table where she and Jett's heads were almost touching as they studied something on her laptop. "How'd it go? Did you have any luck finding a construction crew?"

"We made some good connections. Haven't found the right thing yet," Ben answered.

"Why didn't you ask me for help?" Jett added. "I can recommend some construction managers right around here. Not just in Four Bears."

Jim ignored Jett's question, instead attempting to steady his last nerve by grabbing a glass from the cupboard and filling it at the sink. Turning to the room, he leaned against the counter. "What have you two been up to?"

"We're checking out this software that lets you create a map," Sofia said. "Playing around with what it would look like if you added cabins near the lodge and had paths running in between."

Jim tilted his head, taking in Sofia's smile toward Jett and his brother's grin back. "Looks like you went fishing?"

"We did and I'll have you know," Sofia put her hand on her chest, "I put bait on my own hook and everything."

"Perfect day for fishing." Ben took his glasses out of his shirt pocket and motioned for Sofia to turn the laptop his direction. "Let's see what you got. Look at that, it's 3-D. That's amazing. Jim, you should look at this."

"Maybe later." Jim put his glass in the sink, his back to the room, and stared out the kitchen window.

"I heard you're taking Sofia horseback riding tomorrow."

Jett's words landed like a knife stuck between his shoulder blades. "Actually, I had changed my mind and was going to take her fishing." He turned around, making eye contact with Jett. "Now, I don't think so."

"We should! The great part is you wouldn't have to teach me everything because Jett already did that. Plus I'm not nearly as afraid of worms as I am of horses." Sofia giggled.

Keep a lid on it.

Ben pushed his chair back from the table and winked at Sofia. "Tomorrow is supposed to be another beautiful day. You can never get too much practice fishing." He left the kitchen, calling behind him as he went. "I'm going to wash up and then we should think about putting some supper together."

"It's not all that exciting, but if you want to stay, I could make my famous grilled cheese sandwiches and a fruit salad," Sofia said.

"Not tonight." His voice came out gruff, so Jim added a quick smile then discreetly shook his head at Jett when she wasn't looking.

"Ends up, I have to go too." Jett scooted his chair back, picked up his keys from the counter, and headed out the door. "I'll take a rain check on one of those famous sandwiches."

Sofia pouted. "Okay. I guess that leaves more for me and your dad."

"I'll be back in a minute." Jim headed out the door on the heels of his brother. "Hold up there, slick."

"Ah, Jesus." Jett climbed into his truck and slammed the door. "I didn't do anything, Jim. I took the girl fishing. I didn't know you had plans to do that."

"How'd you know she was here alone today?"

"I didn't. I came by to see if Dad wanted to go to Patsy's Diner."

"And you just happened to have your fishing gear with you and a free afternoon."

"You're starting to piss me off." Jett turned the ignition and revved the engine. "Bro."

Jim put both hands on the roof of his brother's truck, his voice dangerously low as he spoke through the open window. "What happened today, doesn't happen again. You stay away from her. Got it?"

"Or what. Jim?" Jett shouted. "I *told* you, I *didn't* do anything but take her fishing. I may be a drunk, but I'm not a fucking perv."

Jim took a step back, watching gravel and dust spit up as Jett pulled away. Turning back toward the house, he pulled up short at Sofia standing on the back steps.

"What was that all about?"

Jim moved to the bottom of the steps, shrinking inwardly at the stink eye she gave him. "You don't need to be concerned about it."

"So everything's fine. That's why your brother just flew down the driveway like a bat out of hell." She put her hand on her hip. "Why were you mean to him? He was nice to me today."

"I wanted to be the one to take you fishing. Everyone's been riding my ass today about the idea of me taking you horseback riding. Like I was purposely trying to scare the crap out of you."

Fuck. I sound like a whiny brat.

He stomped up the stairs. "Rafe and I stayed up too late drinking, okay? Jett frustrates the shit out of me. I don't know how to deal with him. I was a jerk to my dad." He looked down at her. "Today sucked."

She pressed her lips together and rubbed his arm. "I'm sorry you had a bad day. Are you sure you don't want to have a bite to eat before you leave?"

"No." He gripped the back of his neck. "Thank you. I'm going to go. I need to put myself down for a nap or a time-out."

Thank God that got a tiny laugh.

She opened the door and turned back. "I'm looking forward to spending the day together. Goodnight, Jim."

He walked down the steps and toward his truck, breathing in the night air. The warm yellow light from the kitchen glowed around her image when he returned her wave out the window.

Why do you have to look like everything I want to come home to?

The sky darkened during the drive home to the point he could see only the outline of the foothills. He let the blanket of night calm the stress of his no good, very bad day. Less is more, ghosted like a whisper, a sentiment both his parents subscribed to.

"I miss you, Mom." He said the words out loud as he made the turn past Little Forest Fairgrounds and the lodge, heading toward his house.

A memory from his past landed softly on his heart. Something his mother did to keep him and his siblings encouraged on long family trips when exhaustion from being in the car several hours made everyone squirrely. Inspired, he parked the truck and went into the house. Rafe slept on the couch, a college football game in the last quarter on the television. Jim didn't bother to stop, instead heading upstairs to make a phone call, crossing his fingers his idea would work.

Late the next morning, he texted Sofia that he was about to leave to pick her up for their outdoor day together. Up early, he'd already been to Patsy's Diner and the grocery store. A cooler filled with sparkling water, sandwiches, fruit, and chocolate chip cookies sat in the back of his truck. Blanket, paper plates, napkins…he ran through his mental checklist one more time.

Flowers. Is that too over-the-top? She'll love it. Avoid roses.

En route, he stopped at a garden stand where he knew they had vegetables and flowers for sale.

He agreed with Rafe and his dad that horseback riding hadn't been the best first idea. Still he couldn't stomach, no matter how immature, taking Sofia fishing the day after Jett did. Before drifting to sleep last night, he'd visualized this day being all about Sofia. A drive through the canyon. A short stop at Dragonfly Hill, a local landmark. A picnic next to the Talking Fish River. Plus, the special surprise he hoped she'd be excited about.

Simple. Outdoors. Relaxed.

He passed under the wooden arch on the road

toward the ranch, a bouquet of wildflowers on the passenger seat, smiling at the blue sky and sunshine. Being Sunday, his dad would already at the senior center for the day. He walked up the steps, opening the door to an empty kitchen. "Hello."

"I'll be right out." Sofia called from the back of the house.

Waiting, he held the bouquet in front of him, then quickly tucked it behind his back when footsteps carried down the hallway.

"Hi, Jim." Sofia held her arms out for him to examine what she wore. "Is this going to be okay?"

It wasn't possible to not let his eyes travel down and up her body at the invitation. She wore a yellow t-shirt the color of whipped butter with olive green shorts and tennis shoes. He took in her bare legs. *I don't want to stop seeing them.*

"You look beautiful." His words came out quickly and the immediate blush to her cheeks made his heart speed up. "These are for you." He held out the wildflowers with all the hopes of a boy on his first date.

Stepping toward him, she smiled. "These are so pretty. I'll put them in water." She glanced around the kitchen, then took a vase from the top of the fridge and filled it at the sink.

It pleased him, the way she took her time, carefully arranging the flowers in the vase before setting it at the center of the kitchen table.

"That was really sweet of you. Thank you." Sofia said.

"You're welcome. Are you ready to get going?"

She picked up her camera and a matching yellow sweatshirt from the table. "Ready."

"I thought we'd go on a drive through the canyon," he said, once they were outside. "There's a local spot called Dragonfly Hill where we could make a short stop. One of my mom's sculptures is there. It's a short hike. Then we'll continue further west."

He closed her door, walked around the truck, and climbed in. "We'll be along the river again, so we could stop whenever we get hungry." He gestured toward the back. "I brought some food."

"You've thought of everything." She grinned at him as he helped with her seatbelt. "A perfect day. Helps make up for your bad day yesterday."

He turned the ignition. "That's the plan."

Through the canyon, he glanced away from the road at her profile, taking in her smile. It didn't escape him how neither of them felt a need to fill the silence with mindless chatter. At Dragonfly Hill, they parked and climbed the short rocky path up to where the sculpture of Doc Cindy's sister, Cammie, danced at the top of the hill.

"It's amazing to see one of your mom's pieces outdoors." Sofia circled the young girl, one knee raised as if skipping, a dragonfly at the end of her finger. "It's so joyful."

He put his hand flat on the top of Cammie's head, the bronze hot from the sun. "You can touch it."

"I like what your father said about her wanting people to do that." She put a finger on the dragonfly. "It shows the generosity of her spirit. Sharing her art. I bet you miss her."

"I do." He nodded. "Your photography must feel that way to you."

"I've lost some connection to it since Anthony died. It feels more like the only way for me to make a living now, instead of art. I used to carry my camera absolutely everywhere." She lifted a shoulder. "Now…"

"What do you say we keep moving." He spoke with a gentle tone to soften any abruptness his suggestion might give. "We'll keep driving." It wasn't possible to be sure, but her quick agreement made him wonder if a day without focusing on the past would do them both good.

After another hour on the road, Sofia laughed, a hand on her stomach. "Oh my, that's embarrassing."

"What?"

"You didn't hear that? My stomach growled." Sofia snickered. "I guess I'm hungry. Are you?"

"Yes. There's a good spot not too far ahead, maybe ten minutes. Think you can make it?"

She laughed at his teasing. "I'll try my best."

A few minutes later, he pulled the truck into a small dirt parking lot. It was a short walk down the path to where they could sit by the river. Summer's sweltering heat had dissipated into early fall. He offered her the blanket to bring and carried the cooler, leading the way to a semi-secluded spot, just in case others with similar picnic plans showed up. Spreading the blanket, he waited for her to sit first, then sat and opened the cooler.

"Okay," he said as he pulled items out, "we have sandwiches, fruit, and water." He waved a plastic bag of in the air. "And dessert. Chocolate chip cookies."

She sat, legs outstretched, her natural tan skin a draw to his eyes.

"Turkey with swiss or ham with cheddar?" he asked. "Or we could split them and have some of each."

"Yum. Let's do that. First, I'll have a cookie."

He chuckled, opening the bag so she could pick one out. "Dessert first. A girl after my own heart."

"Yeah, right."

Her tone landed flat and she appeared purposely engrossed in examining the sandwich he handed to her, unwrapping it slowly and avoiding any eye contact.

Say something. She thinks from the other day that you don't even find her attractive.

"You know when we were downtown having lunch…" He paused when she looked up at him then just as quickly away again. "I think I gave you a wrong impression." He put down his sandwich. "Would you please look at me?"

Her lips were pressed together as she made eye contact.

"I think I gave you the wrong impression," he repeated. "As if I don't find you incredibly attractive or that I wouldn't be interested."

She pulled her legs in, sitting cross-legged. "It's okay. We don't have to do a repeat and you don't have to feel bad. I like you. I came off desperate.

I know you like me too. Just … not that way." She mimicked a deep male voice. "Don't feel bad. It's me. Not you. It's complicated." She picked up a grape and popped it in her mouth, muttering words he didn't catch.

"You're so far off, Sofia. Because, unless you tell me no, I'm planning on kissing you today." He opened the cooler and tossed his half-eaten sandwich inside. "If I'm lucky…more than once."

Chapter 13

SHE PAUSED, THE BOTTLE OF sparkling water midway to her lips. "What?"

Jim groaned. "Well, that went about as well as the other day." He pitched his empty water bottle toward the open cooler and missed.

"Stop. No." Sofia changed position getting up on her knees then sitting back on her heels studying him. "That wasn't what I expected you to say."

He's hurt.

"Slow down." She slipped her hand in his and held on, halting his movements as he began packing up. Moving up to her knees again, she gripped his hand for balance. "You'd like to kiss me?"

"Very much."

"But the other day…"

"I was an idiot." He tilted his head. "I think we both know this isn't forever. You're going to leave Colorado, maybe not even that long from now. I'm tired of fighting myself."

"How long have you wanted to kiss me?"

"Since New York."

"Really?" She scooted closer. "That's a long time."

"I have a surprise for you too."

"More than the kiss?" It was a sassy thing to say.

He slipped his hand in her hair and brushed his lips to hers. "It's possible you'll like it even more than my kiss." He held her head at the perfect angle and Sofia moaned when he pressed his mouth firmly, prompting her to open. Her tongue danced with his, another moan escaping when he sucked on her bottom lip. Stopping, he moved his hand to her cheek, his breathing ragged, and rested his forehead to hers.

I need this. I don't want this to stop.

She leaned in, kissing his cheek, chin, neck, then tiny soft kisses along the rim of his ear. Lifting her leg, he situated her so she straddled his lap and pulled her in chest to chest. Her hips pressed forward.

Too much. Too soon. Slow.

As if reading her conflict between head and body, his hands fell to her bare thighs. "Easy, honey. You feel too good." He tucked her hair behind her ear, his eyes filled with lust and awe she instantly felt addicted to. Moving off his lap, she sat cross-legged as he ran a hand over his face and shook his head.

Leaning on her hands behind her, she let her head fall back, closing her eyes. A rolling heat curled her toes and shot straight to her tingling scalp. Sunshine and a gentle breeze fluttered over her skin. Every cell in her body awakened with new energy. "What's the other surprise, because the kissing was really, really good."

"I know coming here, so suddenly, has been hard on you."

The seriousness of his tone made her open her eyes.

"It must feel like life pulled every rug out from under you. That's before you even came to a new place. With me. A stranger."

She grinned. "We're not really strangers now, especially if we've decided to start kissing each other."

His deep laugh, sexy and unnerving, threatened to send her floating up to the clouds.

"We can kiss anytime you want, by the way." He blew out his cheeks, a blank look on his face. "Where was I going with all this?"

"You were going to tell me the surprise," she prompted.

"Right. When me and my brother and sister were little and on long family car trips, my mom would always get us half-way presents."

"What's a half-way present?"

"It's just that. A present you get half-way through a journey, to keep you encouraged. Or in our case, to keep us from killing each other in the back seat of the car."

"I love that idea." She wiggled her eyebrows. "So, I'm getting a half-way present?"

"Last night, I called your parents after I got home."

"You did?" She scooted on her bottom getting close again.

"I invited them to come visit."

"You did?" She repeated, now up on her knees eye-to-eye.

"There's good news and bad news. The bad news is your dad can't come because he has to work. The good news is your mom is flying to Colorado on Thursday, and she's staying until Monday."

She launched herself into his arms as he continued talking. "You and I will pick her up at the airport that afternoon. I made a reservation for her at the B&B in town and there are two beds in the room. That way if you want, you could take a break from the Mannis clan and stay with her during her visit."

She tucked her face against his neck. "Thank you, thank you, thank you."

"Happy?"

"Yes. Best half-way present, ever. Best kisses. Best day."

Sunday night, Sofia called her mom and they talked for an hour about the upcoming visit. It really was the best half-way present and more thoughtful a gift than any object Jim or any man could have given her.

On Monday evening, she stood at the edge of Ben's vegetable garden, the hose in her right hand, watering. Mercy Mountain, solid and distant, rose in front of her. Capturing the image, she sighed deeply and shut her eyes. Sounds of crickets and the wind rustling the leaves sang an evening song to her. A frog croaked. Opening her eyes, she glimpsed intermittent flashes of light in the tall grass.

Fireflies.

She laid the hose on the ground, directing it toward an area of the garden she hadn't soaked, and walked across the yard to the split rail fence. Leaning her arms on the top of the wood post, her mind traveled back in time to ferry rides with Anthony between Manhattan and Staten Island. Eyes closed, Sofia breathed in, the faint smell of water and fish filling her imagination. The sound of the boat engine and murmur of passengers' voices in the background. The breeze off the water pushed her long hair into her face repeatedly. Twelve again, she kept Anthony by her side, her arm protectively around his little waist. He stood, both feet up on the first rung of the iron railing so he could see better. "Mind your brother," her father called from the seats behind them. "When we get home I want to catch lightning bugs," Anthony said in his little boy voice.

Sofia put her chin on top of her hands on the fence, remembering her older sister correction at the time, "Mommy says they're called fireflies." He didn't care. "It doesn't matter, Sissy. We get to see them."

When her phone vibrated, she retrieved it from her back pocket. Walked toward the house, turning off the faucet to the hose on the way, and swiped to read the incoming text.

Jim: Rafe wants to take you to your appointment with Doc Cindy tomorrow. We all know why. Are you okay with him picking you up in the morning?

Sofia: Sounds good, thank you.

Jim: Missed you today.

Sofia: Missed you too.

Jim: Want to have dinner at my place tomorrow?

Sofia: Yes.

Jim: It's a plan. Goodnight, beautiful.

Sofia: Goodnight.

Sofia sat at the kitchen table with Ben, enjoying coffee together on Tuesday morning.

Ben held a finger in the air. "Rafe's here."

"How come you can hear a car coming down the road, way before I do?"

"Years of practice." Ben stood and took both their coffee mugs to the sink. "Are you excited about your mom coming in a few days?"

"So excited." She pushed her chair back and slipped a lightweight jacket over her shoulders. "You should be too. One, you'll get a break while I stay with her at the B&B, and two, she's going to want to cook… *for you*. That's how my mom says thank you." She gestured as if she had a giant belly. "Stuffing people with food."

"We could have everyone out to the ranch on Saturday. Do you think your mom would want to meet the whole family or will that be overwhelming?"

"Are you kidding? She thrives in a crowd. Plus, she's a little jealous of my time here, I think."

Sofia giggled. "She's going to want to check out every Mannis she can."

"You never stop being protective of your children if you're a parent." Ben wiped his hands on a dishtowel. "Have a good appointment. Tell Doc Cindy hello."

"I will."

Once outside, Sofia waved Rafe back when he began to get out of his car. "I got it." She opened the passenger door and got in. "Thanks for giving me a ride."

"Sure thing." Rafe put the car in drive and kept talking. "I'm thinking it would be better if I don't come in to Dr. Wheeler's office *before* your appointment. Instead, I'll be sitting in the lobby when you come out. All casual. Just a friend giving another friend a ride home. What do you think?"

She hid a smirk, keeping her tone neutral. "Good idea. The other way around might seem a bit…"

"Desperate?" Rafe chimed in. "Patriarchal?"

"Patriarchal?"

"Like I'm the older brother type that thinks you need to be walked in there by a man. As if women can't do things on their own. I don't want to come off as that guy."

She smiled. "Good plan."

Rafe glanced away from the road. "Yeah? It's good?"

"Yep." She nodded enthusiastically. "I like it."

Whoa. Talk about wound up.

It was only her second appointment with Dr.

Wheeler. Sofia welcomed the sense of comfortable routine, settling in the same chair as last time and accepting a water bottle when offered.

"How have things gone since last week?" Cindy took a seat across from her and opened a leather notebook on her lap.

"Good. My mom is coming on Thursday for a short visit. I'm excited about that. I wish my dad could come too, but he has less flexibility with his job."

Cindy jotted something on her notepad and glanced up. "That's wonderful. Sounds like you have a close relationship with your parents?"

"Mm, hmm." Sofia nodded. "I do."

"Last time, we were talking about your thoughts around getting back to certain responsibilities you have in New York, with your work and family. Do you want to pick up from there or is there something different you wanted to focus our time on today?"

"I guess I sort of want to pick up there. You mentioned there are methods for reconciling a prior life to a new life after someone dies. I'd be interested in hearing more about those."

"Is this related to your mom's visit coming up?"

Sofia bumped her hand and cast together then apart. "Boom, worlds collide." She laughed. "Perhaps if I have one of these methods in place it will be clear to everyone that I have a plan for the future."

"Having a plan is important to you?"

"I don't know that it always was important." She studied her fingernails for a moment. "It was

Anthony that made plans. He always knew what and where and how."

"And you?"

"I depended on him being that person." Sofia kicked off her shoes and tucked her legs to the side on the chair. "Oops." Her cheeks warmed.

"Be comfortable. Sit any way you like." Cindy waved her hand. "You were saying that you depended on Anthony's plans."

"Thanks. Yes. He always knew what he wanted, whereas I always drifted."

"How did that show up in the family?"

"What do you mean?"

"Was one style more welcome or accepted by the family? Your parents or others?"

She paused, debating how much she wanted to travel this road with a doctor she planned to visit only a few times. Then again, maybe that made Dr. Wheeler the safest person to say out loud what she needed to and be done with it.

"My family is big. Italian. And Spanish. We're traditional. Anthony hit all the marks. He had a good job, a girlfriend he wanted to marry someday, he wanted children. He dreamed of buying our childhood home from our parents someday. He would have lived in New York forever. Then he got sick."

Cindy wrote something in her notebook. "Who relied on Anthony to hit all the marks?"

"My parents," Sofia said. "Don't get me wrong, my family loves me. But I was always the artsy one. I guess because of Anthony balancing things out, I got away with it before."

"And now?"

Sofia shut her eyes and stretched her neck from one side to the other. Taking time to decide whether to say it or not. "And, now, I can't get away with not hitting all the marks. So any methods you have so I can reprioritize my life with that in mind would be welcomed."

Cindy sat forward on the edge of her seat. "When I mentioned methods – and maybe I shouldn't use that word in the future – unfortunately, there isn't a map or a to-do list. I was thinking more about ways to celebrate the life of a person who died for who *they* were, so everyone who loved them can heal in their own lives being who *they* are too."

Sofia twisted the cap on her water bottle one-handed with no success, putting it back on the table with a thud. "Didn't you become a psychiatrist because your sister died?"

"That's true. At least partly. We can't deny our lives are changed as a result of a loved one's death. Quite drastically in fact." Cindy leaned forward, opening Sofia's bottle and setting it down in front of her again.

She crossed her arms and glanced at the clock on the wall. *Five more minutes.* "One of the ways to honor Anthony's life would be to fulfill his dreams as part of my life." Jim's words immediately scrolled like a marquee sign in her head. *That's a nice idea, as long as those dreams match your own.*

Cindy closed her notebook, stood and walked to her desk, riffling through papers, before carrying a document over. "This is an article you might find interesting. It's about linking objects in a meaningful way as a means for honoring someone who has died. It might appeal to you as an artist. Since you're a photographer, photos are an obvious idea, but it can be other objects linked in a way that express and celebrate Anthony's life. We could talk about it next time if you want."

"Okay." Sofia followed Dr. Wheeler out of the office. All six foot two inches of Rafe shot up off the couch in the lobby. Sofia stared, perplexed by a blue bandana he wore on his head and a leather jacket. A long silver key chain hung from the belt of his jeans.

What the heck? Where'd this goofy get-up come from?

"Um, Dr. Wheeler, this is Rafe." She realized she didn't know his last name.

"Mooney. Rafe Mooney." He repeated, clicking his heels, if she wasn't mistaken, and bowing.

Like a freaking butler. Oh Rafe.

Chapter 14

SHORTLY BEFORE NOON, JIM CAME downstairs to find Rafe and Sofia standing in the center of the lodge waiting for him.

"We're here to kidnap you." Sofia clutched Rafe's arm. "Your buddy needs moral support. We can either start playing board games or go day-drinking."

Jim laughed. "These are my choices? He glanced at his watch. "It's only eleven-thirty. Was it that bad?"

Rafe sat on a folding chair with his head in his hands. "I bowed."

Sofia nodded. "Actually, he clicked his heels, *then* bowed to Dr. Wheeler. Like he was the butler to the Queen of England. Everything but kissing the ring."

"Dude, seriously?" Jim barked a laugh as he walked to the card table used as a make-shift desk, tossing his clipboard and pen on it. "How'd your time with Doc Cindy go? Better than Rafe's, I hope?"

"Meh."

"You two are a pair," Jim said. "Am I getting stuck with sad sack all alone as part of this kidnapping, or will you be coming with us?"

Sofia headed toward him with a little extra swing in her walk until she stood toe to toe, looking up. "I'm super competitive when it comes to board games."

He glanced at Rafe with his head still hanging low. Jim snaked his arms around her waist, lifting Sofia off the ground and kissed her. "You haven't seen competitive, sweetheart." He kissed her again, his hands slipping around to cup her bottom.

"Uh, did I miss an episode?" Rafe's voice boomed.

With her arms around his neck, Sofia turned. "Jim and I kiss now."

"You don't say." Rafe grimaced. "That's real sweet and all. However, do you think you could keep the PDA in check at least until I'm shit-faced?"

Jim laughed, letting Sofia slide down his body to stand. "Today's about you and your heartbreak, pal. Are you sure you're okay with this?" He leaned to whisper in Sofia's ear. "It could get a little rowdy once the drinks start flowing."

"Promises, promises." Sofia winked. "Let's get Biker Joe here some relief."

He raised his eyebrows. "I'm going to need to hear more about Biker Joe. I have two rules for this kidnapping." He dug his phone out of his pocket and typed a text hitting send. "It has to be at my house, away from the public eye, no small-town gossip, and we're going to need a fourth if we're playing drinking or board games." Jim grinned when his phone dinged. "All set. Okay, Rafe, you hit the liquor store. Sofia and I will pick up snacks. Kai's bringing the board games."

Sofia jumped up and down. "Kai's coming? Girls versus boys!"

Rafe groaned. "Your sister doesn't like me."

"No, she thinks you're a doofus." Jim rubbed his chin. "Then again, maybe all women do."

"Stop." Sofia smacked him on the arm playfully.

He dug his keys out of his pocket, looking on as she walked over to his best friend and put her hand out, pulling him from his chair. "Come on, Mooney. Let's patch you up so you can try again with Dr. Wheeler on Friday when I have my next appointment."

That's about the kindest offer a person could make. Geez. Rafe's gawking at her, like she just presented him with the sun. I'm not the only one who could fall in love with her.

After a stop at the tiny grocery store near his home, Jim followed Sofia up the steps to his house, carrying a bag filled with chips and dip. "Have you had any alcohol since you've been out here?"

"No, why do you ask? Don't worry, I'm leaving the big drinking to you guys."

"Elevation will make the effects stronger." He unlocked the door and gestured for her to go first.

"Good to know." She faced him, walking backward down the hallway. "I tend to get a little frisky when I drink, so I'll be sure to take it easy."

He shut the door with his foot. "Frisky, huh? I take it back then. You should get hammered."

"Very funny." She leaned against the counter. "While we have a minute, we should consider whether we're letting people in on things, namely your sister."

Jim set down the paper bag and moved directly in front of her, trapping her with his hands on the counter on either side. "Like this kind of thing?" He leaned forward kissing her, then swooped her up, enjoying her yelp. He parted her legs and stepped between. "Wrap yourself around me." He pressed the swell of his body against her, his breath quickening when she shivered. Then sank into the soft warmth of her kiss.

When a car door slammed, he pulled back at the same time she did, her head hitting the cupboard behind her. "Are you okay?"

Sofia rubbed the back of her head and laughed as he lifted her off the counter. "Yes. Where's the bathroom?"

"First door to the left. What'd we decide?"

She tipped her head around the door to the bathroom. "Will Rafe blow our cover anyway?"

He shook his head. "Never."

"Let's keep it on the down low then. That is, if you can manage it."

He grinned, then turned to wave at Kai through the window when she knocked. "Is that a challenge, sweetheart? If so, I accept. We'll see who can keep it under wraps best."

Twenty minutes later, the games were about to begin – beers in hand, boys on one side of the table, girls on the other. Jim scoffed when his sister cracked her knuckles one by one, as if this were a street brawl instead of Monopoly.

"Park Avenue will be mine. Live and learn boys." Sofia picked up the dice and blew on them before tossing.

"We're not in Vegas." Rafe rolled his eyes when she came up with both fives.

"Go, girl." Kai clapped like a madwoman. "Great start."

Ten minutes later, he and Rafe were already in the crapper with a few bucks in the bank and virtually no properties. If he was going to lose, *which he hated,* at least it would be to the gorgeous woman bouncing around in her seat across from him. Pushing back his chair, he took a second to finish his drink. "Anyone need another beer while I'm up?"

"I'll come with you," Sofia said. "Let's bring some chips out too."

As he walked around the corner from the living room, he felt her every step behind him, anticipating the second he could touch her. With no words, he put his hands on her upper arms and backed her against the fridge, his head coming down quick to kiss her hard and hot.

"Oh my God." Sofia whispered as he kissed down her neck and across her collarbone. He smiled against her skin at the way she drew out her words. "This is so…bad."

"Are you bringing the chips or what?" Rafe shouted from the living room.

He raised his head. "Keep your pants on."

"Well, if you insist." Sofia pressed her lips together.

Sassy. Sexy. Flirty. This is going to be a long afternoon.

Over the next two hours, Sofia just happened to make two trips to the kitchen and he three more. By his estimate, they were leaving the table together every ten minutes to make out like teenagers in the kitchen. The last time, they got only as far as the hallway, right around the corner from the living room.

"That's it for me," Kai said at three-thirty. "I have to pick up the kids from school." He chuckled when Kai and Sofia high-fived each other. "Thanks for helping me whup my brother's ass. Bye, Rafe."

"See ya, Kai." Rafe helped Sofia pack up the game as Jim walked his sister out.

"Thanks for coming over."

"It was fun. Oh, and by the way," Kai whispered, "it was pretty obvious what was happening with the fourteen trips to the kitchen together. Rafe and I got quite the little show the last time." She patted his arm with a smirk. "Mirrors reflect, you know. Like the one between the living room and the hallway."

"Damn." He smiled sheepishly.

"I really like her. And I like that you like her. And –"

He interrupted Kai's ramblings, turning her toward the door followed by a gentle push. "Out you go."

Kai turned when she reached the bottom of the steps. "Did Dad tell you he wanted to have everyone out to the ranch on Saturday when Sofia's mom is here?"

"He mentioned it."

"Good. I like having you home and getting to see you often."

"Me too."

"Love you, Jim."

"Love you, Kai."

Jim returned to find an empty living room. The sliding door to the deck in the back was open. The late afternoon breeze threatened to upheave papers on the coffee table. He put a rock he used as a paperweight on top of the bids he still needed to review and opened the screen door, stepping outside. Tan, shapely legs and the sexiest bare feet with red toenails were all he saw over the back of the chaise lawn chair.

He came around the chair, gesturing for her to scoot over. "Where's Rafe?"

"He's taking a nap." She lay next to him on her side.

"Kai knows."

Sofia put a hand on the middle of his chest and sat up. "How?"

"She and Rafe were apparently counting the number of times we left the kitchen together. She says it was fourteen."

"It wasn't *that* many times." Sofia brushed her hair behind her ear and laid her head on his shoulder. "Well, that's embarrassing."

He tipped her face up with a finger under her chin and kissed her softly. "Not to me. I feel like the luckiest man alive every time I touch you."

Her arm slipped around his middle, squeezing as she laid her head down again. "We're getting good at kissing." She sat up again. "My lips are swollen."

Jim thought he'd die from his instant hard watching her run a finger over her lips.

"What's the plan when your mom gets here?"

"Mm, good question." She put a leg over his and molded herself to the side of his body before glancing up. "I tell my mom everything."

He ran his hand along her side, squeezed her ass gently, then left his hand resting on her naked thigh. "Everything?"

Her fingers fiddled with the buttons on his shirt as she nodded.

"You'll tell her we kissed?" He leaned to kiss the delicate skin at her collarbone. His hand hovered in the air before cupping her breast when she nodded. "And that I touch you here?" He bent his head, his finger tugging the V-neck to her shirt lower as he dragged his lips across the soft skin at the top of her breast. "You'd tell?" Eyes closed, she nodded. His hand slipped under her shirt unclasping her bra. He brushed his thumb across her nipple. "This too?"

"You're making me crazy." Sofia sighed. "Touch

me."

Jim shifted her flat on her back, up on his arms looking down. "Show me where, sweetheart." He held his breath as she slowly dragged the hem of her shirt over her stomach and above the loose cups of her pink bra with black polka dots. She bit her bottom lip, eyes fixed on his. He slid his hands beneath her, encouraging her to arch her back so her bra fell open and her breasts were revealed to him. Lowering his head he pressed her nipple between his lips. Fluttering his tongue, he licked and pulled. He lifted up again, his hand running along one of her thighs. She pulled both legs up, cradling his body intimately. Lowering again, he repeated his ministrations on her other breast.

He let go her breast with a soft pop and left a row of kisses across her stomach. "We need privacy." He mumbled, kissing both her breasts again and laying his head on her chest. "I can't get enough." He lifted his head, wanting her understanding of how much he wanted her and how much that meant to him.

"I want to be with you too." Her sexy smile set his world spinning, her fingers through his hair pure heaven. Her words.

Perfection.

"Is this the last of the beer?" His eyes met hers at Rafe's voice coming from inside the house. He appreciated his buddy's discretion by announcing his arrival. Leaning on his elbow, he clasped Sofia's bra again and pulled her shirt down.

Rafe opened the screen door and stepped out.

"You two lovebirds want to get a pizza?"

Two pieces in, Sofia pushed her plate away, rubbing her belly. "I'm stuffed."

"You're a lightweight." Rafe folded his slice of pizza and shoved another bite in his mouth.

"You eat pizza like a New Yorker."

"I eat like a man."

Jim wiped his mouth enjoying the two of them sparring. He might otherwise be jealous. Somehow knowing the people he liked also liked each other…well, it worked. "That reminds me. Tell me about this Biker Joe persona."

Jumping up from her chair, Sofia became more animated than he'd ever seen her.

She lifted her arms in front of her, as if about to tell the best ghost story to a group of campers. "So, Rafe picks me up from your Dad's, right? He's wearing a white t-shirt, jeans and sunglasses. Normal, right?"

Damn, she's cute.

He nodded, laughing as embarrassment swept across Rafe's face.

"We get everything planned." Sofia motions her hand like a wave. "We're driving."

"What are you driving, a boat?"

"Shh, listen. Rafe is going to be in the lobby after my appointment and then I can facilitate his love connection with Doc Cindy." At this point, Sofia bent forward with a hand on her knee cracking up.

This woman. Funny too.

Standing up straight and clearing her throat, she barely managed to get any words out. Stumbling forward, and much to his pleasure, Sofia took a seat on his lap before continuing.

"Dr. Wheeler and I come out of her office. And there's Biker Joe with a blue bandana on his head, leather jacket and a ridiculously long silver key chain hanging from his pants."

"I don't like either of you," Rafe announced.

"Then what happened?" Jim asked, slipping his arm around her waist.

"Alright, Miss Sassafras." Rafe pushed his chair back, walking over and putting his hand out. "Let's act out what happens next. I'll be me."

"Otherwise known as dumbass," Jim quipped as he lifted Sofia from his lap.

"Shut up, dipshit. Sofia, you'll be Doc Cindy."

After making a goofy face, she headed toward the other side of the patio.

"Where are you going?" Rafe asked.

"I'm making my entrance to the lobby."

Jim moved to the edge of his seat, prepared for an Oscar-winning performance. From across the patio, Sofia walked, flinging her hair with one hand and struck a pose with her hip jutting out.

Like a fucking supermodel.

"Hi," she said in a sultry voice Jim hoped he'd hear next time they were alone. "I'm Dr. Wheeler. People around these parts call me Doc Cindy."

His dick throbbed against his zipper.

Stand down.

Enthralled, he looked expectantly to his buddy.

"Mooney," Rafe shouted, grabbing Sofia's outstretched hand and kissing the back of it. "Rafe Mooney at your service." He added, clicking his heels together and bowing.

An hour later, Jim carried the empty pizza box into the house and dropped it into the recycle container.

"Want me to ride along?"

"Not really." Jim laughed at Rafe's question as he helped Sofia maneuver her jacket over her cast. "When are you free of this thing, honey?"

"I hope tomorrow. Kai told me I could stop by the clinic."

"Goodnight, Mooney," Sofia added with a salute to Rafe. "Until Friday my friend."

"Until Friday."

He drove Sofia home and kept it simple with a walk to the door and a quick kiss. He examined his vibrating phone when he got back in his truck.

Rafe: Even though you and your woman made fun of me... I made plans to be in Four Bears tomorrow night.

Jim: All night?

Rafe: Yep. Make the most of it.

Jim: Thanks

Rafe: Hey, I remembered something from the other day. Your dad had me take a sculpture to the senior center gardens after your mom died. She wanted it near the river.

Chapter 15

WEDNESDAY MORNING, SOFIA SLEPT IN late, took a long shower and texted her mother to confirm the time she and Jim would pick her up at the airport the next day. The day started cloudy, but changed to a blue-sky day by eleven, when she finally emerged from her room.

"Hey, Kai," she said to Jim's sister standing at the kitchen counter. "I didn't know you were coming by today."

Over her shoulder, she smiled. "I brought some food to put in Dad's freezer. He's out in the barn. I was going to make him a sandwich for lunch. Do you want one?"

"No thanks. We ended up getting pizza last night. I'm still full."

"That was fun yesterday. I love having Jim around all the time. I can even stand Rafe."

Sofia laughed and sat at the table. "How do you feel about me and Jim, you know…"

Kai took two pieces of bread out, spinning the bag and refastened it with a twist-tie. "It's none of my business."

"Can I ask you something?"

"Sure. What's up?"

"How did you know you wanted to have children? I mean, did you always want them or was it like your biological clock ticking?"

"It definitely wasn't a biological clock ticking since Will came along early." Kai wrapped Ben's sandwich in plastic wrap, put it on a plate and stuck it in the refrigerator. "I wasn't expecting to get pregnant so young." She pulled out a chair, sitting kitty-corner to Sofia. "How much has Jim told you about what it was like after our mom died?"

"Not a lot. He told me your ages when she passed away. He mentioned your dad was lost."

Kai nodded and glanced toward the back door as if making sure Ben wasn't about to come inside. "That's a nice way to put it. Dad pretty much checked out for a few years."

"He left?" Sofia's voice rose an octave.

"No." Kai patted her hand reassuringly. "He didn't literally leave, but he was depressed and went through the motions of being a father, but that was about it."

"I'm so sorry. That must have been devastating for all of you."

"It was. Mom was…special." Kai smiled. "I got her the longest. We all kind of scattered, running from grief in different directions. Jim ran off to the Army. Jett's still running. My way was boys. Plural."

"Not Leo, I take it?"

"No. Leo wasn't in the picture yet. I did meet him the same year I got pregnant. He's ten years older than me. I think he liked me from the start. He was a nurse at the hospital where Will was born. I grew up fast by becoming a mother, but it still took time to go from being a girl to a woman."

Sofia smiled when Kai blushed a soft pink. "Leo seems like a wonderful husband and father."

"He is." Kai nodded. "So, yeah. I don't know if it was a conscious thing either way, at least with the first baby. Once Leo and I were married, we talked about it and both wanted kids. Leo's the only father Will has ever known. Not long after, Jocelyn was born and the twins. We thought we were done. Then came Suze."

"Is it hard having a special needs daughter?"

"It's hard having five kids. Period. Suze has her unique set of challenges. We all do, don't we?"

"I guess that's true," Sofia agreed.

"Would you like to have kids someday?"

She expected the question. Naturally, it would come up. Despite that, she wasn't prepared. "I'm not sure." She cringed, kicking herself for not practicing a better response. "I didn't think about it until my brother died. I feel like I owe it to my parents."

"Is that what they expect?"

"They'd never come right out and say it, but..."

"Maybe it's something you could speak with your mom about when she's here?"

"Maybe."

She and Kai both looked at the door when

Ben's boots thumped on the back steps. "If you ever want to talk more, let me know," Kai murmured.

"Thank you."

A late afternoon rain shower left everything muggy when the sun broke through and steamed the earth. Sofia read, enjoying a quiet day with Ben as he dozed in his recliner. When her phone vibrated and Jim's name appeared on the screen, she picked up and whispered hello as she moved down the hall to her bedroom. "Hold on. Your dad's asleep. Okay, I'm in my room. How did work go today?"

"Good. I'm on my way over."

"Do you want to stay for dinner tonight?"

"What are we having?"

"That's not polite," Sofia said with a chuckle. "You can't ask that before you say yes or no."

Jim's deep laugh rang out. "Yes, I'd like to stay."

"We're having lasagna. It's heating in the oven."

"Sounds perfect. I was hoping you'd come back home with me after."

"Sure, I could come over for a while."

"To stay over. Rafe's in Four Bears for the night."

"Are you asking me what I think you're asking me?"

"Yes."

She loved his directness and answered without pretense. "Okay."

"That was easy."

"Hey, be careful or you won't get any pie for dessert."

He groaned. "You made pie too? What kind?"

"I made two. Strawberry-rhubarb and blueberry."

"My favorite is blueberry with a dollop of sex on the side."

Sofia got up from sitting on the edge of her bed, moving the curtain aside to look out the window. "Only a dollop?" she asked as his truck pulled in front of the house and he got out. Careful not to wake Ben, she tip-toed down the hall to the kitchen to greet Jim.

He opened the door, his phone still to his ear. "You made a whole pie, right? So one dollop per piece."

She placed her phone on the counter, slipped her arms around him and leaned back. "That's a lot of pie."

"One nibble at a time," he whispered against her smile, then kissed her breath away.

She stepped out of his arms when the timer on the oven went off.

"Is dinner ready?" Ben called from the living room.

"Yes, and we have a guest." Sofia smiled when Ben opened the swinging door to the kitchen. "Jim's here."

"Hey, son. Lasagna first. Then pie." Ben rubbed his hands together.

"I'm all about pie." Jim winked in her direction.

"I'm going to wash up. Be right back."

Sofia rolled her eyes when Ben left the room.

"You get to figure out how to explain why I'm staying at your house tonight."

"We'll just tell him the truth." Jim answered.

"No. We. Will. Not." Sofia laughed. "You have to come up with a reason."

Jim popped an olive from the relish tray on the table into his mouth. "He's going to know."

She walked over and poked him in the side. "Think of something. We can't just tell him." She backed up until her hip met the counter, giggling as Jim tickled her waist.

"Tell me what?" Ben asked as he came into the kitchen again.

Jim faced her with a silly smirk on his face only she could see. "Um," she peeked around him to look at Ben, "Jim says I have to stay at his house tonight because of the early start we need to make for picking up my mom from the airport tomorrow."

"Oh." Ben pulled his chair at the table and sat down. "That makes sense. More pie for me, then."

"Nice try, Dad." Jim gave her waist a squeeze and turned around. "We'll take ours with us."

"Humph," Ben responded with a chuckle.

She opened the oven and put the lasagna on the stove. "I'll be right back to serve. I just need to wash up myself. It's so great having my cast off and being able to use both hands again."

At dinner, Jim listened as Sofia explained more about a linking object project Doc Cindy gave her an article about. She planned to talk to her mom during her visit about using her photography of her brother's football teams over the years along with family photos. Sofia shook her head. "When Dr. Wheeler first gave me the article to read, I sort of resented the whole idea."

"Why's that?" Ben asked.

"It sounded stupid somehow. Like making a scrapbook about someone that died. But then I thought about what your family is doing with the lodge. And it's so much bigger than a one-time event like a funeral."

Jim took in the way his dad was nodding. It didn't take a genius to understand his brother's ideas for the lodge offered a similar opportunity. Literally, Jett was linking how to set up the property, including the lodge and new cabins, with the family and their mother's legacy. *I get it. I'll find a way to work with Jett.*

"They, and we, go on," Ben said. "Life goes on."

"Exactly." Sofia smiled. "Somewhere along the way, we'll lose count of how many kids benefit from Anthony's scholarship."

"And the Mannis family will eventually lose count of how many people enjoy time together at Mercy Mountain Lodge," Jim added.

"I can't wait for that day."

Ben patted Sofia's hand. "Me too."

After dinner, Jim rinsed dishes as Sofia was in her room packing an overnight bag. His father sat at the table, enjoying a slice of each type of pie.

"Did I ever tell you how your mother stayed

with me at the ranch her second night in Ashnee Valley?"

"Mom did?" Jim turned his head, his hands still under the running water.

"It was scandalous at that time in such a small town. Lucky for me, your mother was…" Ben paused to wipe his mouth with his napkin "…ahead of her time."

"I guess so." Jim laughed. "And she asked *you* to marry *her*. Who did that in the 70's?"

"Who does that now?" Ben said. "She was one of a kind."

He turned off the faucet and dried his hands on a towel. "Is that why you never remarried?"

"It would be easy to say yes to that question." Ben scratched the top of his head.

Jim sat down at the table. "But?"

"I regret not finding someone after your mother died. For a long time, I convinced myself it would be like cheating on her. Or to bring someone else into my life would disrespect her as your mother. I wasn't confident I could withstand happiness again. That sounds counterintuitive, I know."

"Why are you telling me this?"

"You understand things more clearly at my age. I see a lot of myself in Sofia. She's sorting through how to go forward herself, plus she wants to carry what would have been Anthony's life on her shoulders too. I did this when my parents passed away, focusing only on raising my younger brothers. I did this when your mother died, focusing only on trying to keep you kids from falling off a cliff. Meanwhile, I did."

"We all got through it the best we could. I don't want to hurt Sofia. It'll be hell, but I'll stay away from her, if that's what you're telling me is best."

"I'm not telling you that." Ben sighed. "And she's not the only one I worry about. I notice how you look at her. It's funny, it took her coming here for me to grasp how much I've hidden behind loyalty to your mother's memory so I wouldn't have my heart broken again. Now I'm alone. I wouldn't want that for any of you kids. Does any of this make sense?"

"It does."

His father pushed his plate forward. "Don't ever forget you deserve happiness. Fight for it if you need to."

It was dark by the time he carried Sofia's overnight bag to the truck. She followed, balancing two plastic containers filled with pie.

"Precious cargo," he said, taking the containers so she could get in the truck.

She laughed at his silly joke. "Oh, you mean the pie."

Jim closed her door, stowed the pie on the floor in the backseat, got in and buckled his seatbelt. His father's words weighed on his mind as he drove under the Mannis Ranch arch and turned onto the main road. "So, do you think we should talk about anything? First?"

Sofia tilted her head and smiled his direction. "First?"

He responded to her faux innocence with a knowing look. "Before we jump each other. Should we talk about anything?"

"Oh, that. I'm safe. No STDs. You should wear a condom. Okay, your turn."

Jim shook his head. "Same. That wasn't quite where I was going. I meant emotionally. This will change things between us. How do you feel about it?" He glanced her way when she rested her hand on top of her head and closed her eyes.

"When were you first attracted to me?"

"You're a stunning woman. I'd say the moment I met you."

"That's based on looks only. I mean, real attraction."

"I knew what you meant." Jim smiled. "At the cookout at Kai and Leo's house."

Sofia put her hands in her lap and wrinkled her nose at him. "When I cried?"

"Well, not that exact moment. It was when you were sitting on the floor with all those crazy barrettes Suze put in your hair. You didn't care about looking silly. I don't know, I guess that image stuck in my mind. Plus, I was proud of you. You were having a hard day and you stuck it out."

"That's sweet."

"How about you? When were you *really* attracted to me?"

"On the airplane."

"Early." Jim grinned. "Wow."

"For the first time in weeks I didn't feel heartbroken. You made me laugh and we were a little flirty. It felt normal. I felt safe." His heart beat hard when she turned to him with a shy smile. "We weren't each other's past or each other's future. There was nowhere else to be than right there. Just us."

Us.

He pulled the truck to a stop in front of his house, got out, and came around to open her door. "Come inside." He put his hand out. "Tonight, there's only you and me."

Chapter 16

SOFIA LEANED ON THE KITCHEN doorframe as Jim set the pie on the table and put dinner leftovers in the refrigerator.

Facing her again, he asked, "Would you like me to get a fire going on the patio?" He rocked his head side to side. "Take things slow, build our way there."

She smiled. "I'd like that."

"I want to show you something first before we go outside." He offered his hand, leading her through the living room to a small study at the back of the house. "I found my mother's sketches and notes. Jett reminded me they were here in the house, not at the lodge."

He let go of her hand then pulled a large banker's box from beneath the desk and placed it on top.

"Have you seen these before?" Sofia asked, moving closer as he lifted the lid.

He shook his head. "I do remember she kept them. Sometimes she'd get an idea in the middle of dinner or whatever and wander off." He chuckled. "She kept a notebook on her bedtable, too, for middle-of-the-night inspirations."

Jim handed her a notebook and then picked up another himself.

"Do you have a favorite of hers?" Sofia asked as she flipped through the pages of sketches and notes. "You never answered that when we were at the lodge."

He held the book up to a page with a line drawing of the hawk with a rabbit in its talons. "Remember this one?"

"I do. It looks just like the drawing." Sofia came to stand next to Jim. "What does her note say."

"This one may upset Kai." Jim read. "By the date here, Kai would have only been about nine at the time."

"But she didn't say that about you. That you'd be upset."

"It must have been when Kai went through her 'I want to be a veterinarian' stage. Animals dying, especially a bunny, was not her thing."

"Back to your favorite, which is it?"

"It wasn't in the basement. It's not typical of her usual stuff because it's not wildlife. I mean, I know she did the sculpture of Cammie that's on Dragonfly Hill, but she didn't do a lot of people. It's me reeling in a fish, leaning back a little with my arms raised."

She smiled at his gestures for casting a line in the water then mimicking the fight to bring a fish in.

"We should try to find her notes on it."

"That could take a while." He pulled sketchbook after sketchbook out of the box and stacked them on the desk. "I have other plans tonight."

"Good point." Sofia placed the book she held on the stack. "How about I pour us each a glass of wine?"

"Perfect."

Sofia turned on the light above the stove when she entered the kitchen, then came back to flip off the too-bright overhead light. With the window open, she could hear crickets chirping in the dark. After she poured two glasses of red wine, she turned to head back only to find Jim leaning on the doorframe. "Can I dance with you?"

Sofia handed him his glass and then picked hers up from the table and took a sip. "You want to dance here in the kitchen?"

"More than anything." Jim walked around her to the counter and turned on the radio. "I need to hold you."

She set down her glass and waited, her chest rising with nervous breaths until his hand settled on her lower back, pulling her flush with him.

"No matter what happens." He bent his head and whispered in her ear. "Let me love you, sweetheart, with all of me tonight."

Sofia looked into his eyes as they swayed. "I wouldn't be here if that's not what I wanted too. When this song is over, will you take me upstairs and show me?"

"Now." He flipped off the radio. "Bed."

When he picked her up, she wrapped her legs around him, loving the fact she reduced this big, strong, smart man to one-word primitive expressions.

He carried her up the steps. Only a soft glow from a bedside lamp lit the bedroom. They undressed in silence, her hands on his chest as he lifted his shirt over his head. His lips on her neck as she slipped off her jeans. Naked, she scooted backward to the middle of the bed, his gaze darting with every slight movement. She rubbed one foot over the other.

"Let me see you." His eyes lowered as he put one knee on the bed, prowling as she moved her legs apart. Hovering, he leaned to kiss her, his finger skimming intimately. "So soft." He murmured against her lips. "Wet."

She turned her head to the side, heat creeping along her neck and cheeks.

"Hey." His hand gentle, he turned her to face him directly. "Are you embarrassed?"

She lifted a shoulder her teeth tugging her bottom lip.

He kissed her forehead, her warm cheek, her neck. "Don't you know how sexy that is? The fact that you want me as much as I want you. It makes me crazy."

She wrapped her arms around him, giggling as he playfully nuzzled her neck. When he pushed himself up, pulling away from her embrace, she whimpered.

"I plan to explore every dip and swell." He moved to the end of the bed. His ascent began at the tips of each toe, moving to kiss the top of her feet and her ankles. His warm hands kneaded the muscles of her calves.

"The first dip." He bent one of her legs the slightest bit, his tongue touching the back of her knee. He did the same to her other knee before straightening her legs again, running his hands up, his thumbs pressing the delicate flesh of her inner thighs before pushing her legs farther apart. Rising on his arms, he grinned above her. "Now these dips are some of my favorites." He skimmed his thumb along the indentation at the top of her thighs. Open-mouthed he followed with his lips along the same route, his warm breath traveling over her sex. One side, then back. She raised her hips.

"Is there something you wanted?" A grin tugged at the corners of his lips.

"You missed a swell." Sofia raised her arms above her head and stretched, arching her back.

"So helpful." He growled.

He placed a firm kiss at the very spot that hid her feminine nerves and she gasped, frustrated when he stopped.

"Patience, sweetheart."

His hand slid from her hip up to her waist. At her breasts he bent, resting his cheek gently. She ran her fingers through his hair. Lovingly tender, romantic, and oh so contented.

Jim.

"You're beautiful." His voice was deep and ragged as he kissed her collarbone. His erection pressed against her leg and she wasn't sure if she would ever get enough of this moment. This man.

"Come inside." She felt his smile against her

neck before he raised his head. Her hands on his face, she pulled him in, pouring everything into her kiss.

Slowly she guided him to her, caressing gently, stopping momentarily as he slipped on a condom. So slick with desire he entered in one excruciatingly slow, deep thrust. His eyes closed, she gave herself over to him too, intoxicated with the way his hands gripped her thighs, the way his hips undulated. Rocking with his rhythm and his pleasure as much as her own. Eyes open again, he kissed her, resting his hands by her shoulders. She slowed their movements and led the pace before he surged forward again.

"More." She pleaded as he pushed farther inside her. "Deeper."

"Hold on, honey." He brought his arms under her thighs, lifting her knees up and around him as his movements became urgent. She enveloped him, so close with every thrust.

"Oh God." An orgasm pulsed suddenly, her inner muscles squeezing. Stiffening, he uttered a loud oath and buried his head in her neck.

She moaned with him when he eventually pulled out, dispensing of the condom and turning off the light before wrapping his arms around her.

"Let's sleep, firefly. It won't be long before I want you again."

Jim awoke when he could no longer feel her heat beside him. Sofia sat cross-legged, pie plate on her lap, a blanket wrapped around her shoulders.

"You're right," she mumbled around a mouth full, her teeth purple, "pie with a dollop of sex is the best."

He put his arm over his eyes. "Woman you have worn me out."

"You want some pie, old man, so you can get your energy back?"

He peeked out from under his arm as she took another heaping bite. *Damn. You are the cutest thing I've ever seen.* "Old man?"

"You are several years older than me."

"Like seven years. What I lose in a sprint, I can make up for in a marathon. You have to give me that after last night."

"Definitely." She enthusiastically said, digging her fork back into the pie.

"I want some." He sat up against the headboard and took the pie plate from her hands, chuckling when she frowned at him. Setting the pie on the night table, he reached for her, lifting her until he situated her straddling his lap. He kissed her, enjoying the newfound blueberry taste.

It took all of four seconds to grow hard as she moved against him. "God, honey, you're going to kill me." She stopped at his words and he delighted in the mischievous look sweeping across her face. Leaning, she picked up the pie and brought it back between them, taking a large forkful and offering it to him.

"You'll be proud to know I can do more than one thing at a time." She wiggled on his lap. "Sort of like walking and chewing gum."

"This is nothing like walking and chewing gum." He opened his mouth taking the bite offered. "It's pie and fucking and the closest we'll ever get to heaven on earth."

Her blanket slipped from her shoulders, her breasts shaking as she laughed. "Oh my." She glanced down at his hard on. "We really need to do something about that."

He lifted the plate from her hands and put it back on the table. "Let's lose the pie." Sliding down on the bed, his hands gripped her hips as she hovered, lowered, lifted and rocked.

Chapter 17

JIM GLANCED TOWARD SOFIA ON the passenger side and put his hand palm up on the car seat between them. When she intertwined her fingers with his, all felt right in his world. The morning sun coming through the windshield, the cool September breeze, making love last night.

"You're wonderful," he said taking in her soft smile. "In every way. You know that, right?"

"Last night was pretty great."

"*Pretty* great?" He chuckled with her when she laughed and squeezed his hand.

"It was amazing. I'm feeling…I don't know. Shy, maybe?"

"With me?"

"Shy about it. About us. I have a lot of thoughts."

"And here I am only thinking about the fact that it's a real shame you'll be spending the next several nights at the Sinclair B&B with your mom."

"It totally stinks," Sofia said on a dramatic wistful sigh that made his ego swell and a deep laugh escape.

He let go her hand to make a turn onto Moon Ridge Road, heading around Mercy Mountain toward the highway to the airport.

She opened the thermos of coffee he'd prepared for their drive and poured a small amount in the cup. "Do you want some first?"

"You go ahead. I'll have some next. Are you looking forward to seeing your mom?"

Sofia held the cup to her lips and blew on the hot liquid before answering. "I am."

The smell of fresh coffee wafted under his nose and he returned her beaming smile.

"It's been like another world here," she continued. "I could use some Mom time. I'm not sure how it will go when I tell her I'm staying longer. Anyway, these few days are going to go fast."

He kept his eyes on the road and nodded. "You don't have to feel obligated to anything but spending time with her. Even dinner Saturday at the ranch. That's not set in stone."

"Are you kidding? That will be my mom's favorite part. We're going to knock everyone's socks off with her authentic Spanish cooking."

"Just the thought of that makes my stomach growl," Jim said. "What else do you have planned?"

Now that they were off the curvy canyon road and on the highway, Sofia poured another cup of coffee, offering it to him.

"I'm glad you asked. Are you okay if I take Mom to the lodge? I want to take some more pictures, especially now that I have your mother's art journals from last night. I'm not sure if that will happen on Friday or Saturday though."

"Sure. The key is under the plant near the front door. But you don't need to do that. I don't expect you to be working on the before pictures while she's here or any other work related to the lodge."

"I know you don't. I want to though. I'm excited about the idea of the linking project Doc Cindy suggested. It was supposed to be a way to work through grief about Anthony, but my focus is leaning toward how my photography can help shape something for the Mannis family's future. About your dad, about your mom's art, about you, Jett, and Kai building your futures around the lodge. By the way, I have another appointment with Dr. Wheeler tomorrow and Mom is going to come to that."

"What about your future?" Jim asked, looking over at her profile as she stared out the window.

"That is what I'm talking about. One more shot. I could see the lodge restoration even becoming a book."

"What does one more shot mean?"

"Before other things." She turned his direction. "Before I do the things everyone does." Sofia waved her hand and laughed a little too hard for his liking before staring out the window again. "Settle down, have kids. All that. It's going to be a full court press coming from my parents whenever I do go home. You wouldn't want to move back to New York by any chance, would you?"

"I'm afraid my New York days are over."

"I know. I was kidding."

"Was it a mistake for me to invite your mom?"

"No, not at all." Sofia shook her head.

He debated whether to push the elephant in the room completely out in the open. "Do you want to talk about this more?"

Sofia shrugged. "About what more?"

Okay.

Jim took the next exit off the highway and turned left, following the sign to the arrival deck at the airport.

"Hey, when you see Rafe later, will you let him know he won't need to drop me off for my doctor appointment tomorrow?" Sofia said.

"He'll be crushed," Jim said, trying to lighten the mood as he pulled the car to the curb.

"Yeah, well, life doesn't always work out the way we want." Sofia pointed toward Mia Russo walking through the double doors to the outside. "There she is." She opened her door and jumped out. "Mom!"

He put the car in park, popped the trunk, and got out, watching as the two women embraced. He'd forgotten how much mother and daughter looked alike. Same height, build, long brown hair.

"You're thinner. Are you eating enough?" Sofia's mother asked as they walked back toward the car.

"Hi, Mrs. Russo." Jim smiled. "It's good to see you again."

"You too. You can call me Mia, by the way."

He reached for her bag and put it in the trunk.

"Thank you, Jim. Now give me a hug too."

He leaned forward, patting Sofia's mother on the back as she hugged him.

Sofia opened the car door. "I'm going to sit in the back with Mom so we can talk."

"You got it. Enjoy each other. I'll just drive."

The ride back to Ashnee Valley was more awkward than he anticipated. He couldn't put the window down without the breeze being too windy for the backseat. He couldn't turn on the radio or they wouldn't be able to hear each other.

"Jim, how's your father doing?" Mia asked at one point.

"All good. You should ask your daughter too since she's been living with him."

He loved hearing Sofia's enthusiasm as she spoke about his father. "Ben is great, Mom. He makes me breakfast. We garden. I've even fed his chickens and horse. In the evenings we read or listen to country music. It's been relaxing. Ashnee Valley is an entirely different speed than New York City."

"He makes you breakfast? Sofia, that's something you should do for him, not the other way around."

"Dad's a rancher, Mrs. Russo," Jim chimed in. "He's going to have breakfast going long before Sofia's even awake."

It was impossible to avoid locking eyes with Sofia in the rearview mirror after his idiotic response to her mother's scolding. *Sorry.* He mouthed the word with a grimace.

Okay, moron, pretend you're not listening to every word of their conversation.

"How's Dad doing?"

"You know your father. Work keeps him sane. He's been in touch with the high school to set up a football scholarship. It won't be big dollars, but it will be something in Anthony's name."

"That's wonderful, maybe I can contribute? Dr. Wheeler has this idea..."

"You don't even have a job at the moment." Jim cringed when Sofia's mother interrupted mid-sentence. "It's something your father is doing. Carrying the family name forward is important."

"It wouldn't have to be money. I could do something with all the photographs I've taken of Anthony and his players over the years."

"That's a nice idea. Why don't you mention that the next time you talk to him? Oh, you know who we see every weekend? Valerie. We sit with her at the Friday night games."

Jim took in the clouds forming over the mountains. "Looks like we might get a little rain." He rolled his shoulders at the lack of response from the backseat.

"You're still going to football games?"

"Yes. Valerie and your brother remind me so much of your father and I when we first met. Anyway, I think it helps for us to be there. Anthony gave her a ring. Did you know he'd done that?"

Jim rubbed the back of his neck. Unable to withstand the awkward conversation, he started fiddling with the radio, adjusting the station and volume. "Sorry ladies, I need to interrupt for a moment and catch the weather report. Just give me a minute."

"That's fine, I'll take in the view," Mia said. "I've never been to Colorado. It's beautiful."

He took a deep breath and kept his attention on the road until his heart couldn't stop his gaze from lifting and meeting Sofia's watery eyes in the mirror.

After the longest hour and a half drive of his life, he finally pulled the car in front of the Sinclair B&B and cut the engine. "Here we are."

"This little town is charming," Mia said.

"Just wait until we drive through the canyon to get to the lodge," Sofia responded. "I've never seen anything like the mountains around here."

"Speaking of driving, I'm going to leave Kai's car with you ladies. She's on her way over from work to give me a lift home. Kai's my sister," Jim added for Mia's benefit. "We swapped vehicles, so she has my truck today. You'll meet her family at the ranch on Saturday."

"Sofia told me she has five kids." Mia smiled. "I'm looking forward to meeting everyone. Your whole family has done so much for ours."

They got out of the car and Jim lifted the suitcase from the trunk. "I couldn't have accomplished what I have already on the lodge without your daughter's help, so it all has worked out well." Standing behind Mia, Sofia shook her head in his direction, only moving her lips. *It's okay.*

Jim turned and led the way up the short walk

and front step of the B&B. He set the suitcase down and opened the door for Sofia and her mother to go first. With Mia occupied checking in, he offered his goodbyes and headed outside.

"I'll be right back, Mom. I forgot to ask Jim something." Sofia descended the steps behind him. When she grabbed his hand, he followed, letting her pull him across the grass and around the corner to the side of the house.

"It's okay." She stared up at him.

"What the fuck was that in the car? That passive aggressive shit?" He grabbed the back of his neck, a headache coming on.

"She's out of her element. It's just a reaction to feeling out of control of the circumstances."

"Are you sure?"

"I'm positive. Listen, I know my mother. She's very comfortable on her own turf. We'll find our footing again when it's just the two of us. No offense."

Jim shrugged. "None taken, I guess."

"There is something you could do that would help." Sofia pushed him backward until his back rested against the side of the house. "Kiss me."

That I can do.

Slipping one hand in her hair and the other on her backside, he molded her entire length along his body and covered her lips with his. "I'm going to miss you." He said a few minutes later when he ended the kiss and walked with her to the front of the B&B.

"Yes, you are." She waved at Kai arriving in his truck. "See you in a couple days. Don't worry."

He took his sister up on her offer to drive, staring out the window with little conversation between them as they headed through town.

"Are you all right?" Kai asked eventually.

He cleared his throat. "I'm fine. Just thinking about all the stuff I want to get done in the next couple days. Could we stop for a second at the senior center gardens? Rafe told me one of Mom's sculptures is there. Do you have time?"

"Sure. It's the angler one. I may stay in the car if that's okay. I need to return a call to Suze's doctor." Kai looked his way with a smile. "It's not like I haven't seen that sculpture a million times already."

Jim got out and headed down a path along the gentle slope that led to an area that ran along the Talking Fish River. At the bottom of the hill, he turned looking back at the old folks home, a one-story white building with the tall windows. Lifting his hand, he acknowledged Kai's gesture out the car window, pointing the direction he should take to find the sculpture.

Only a few steps more and he found himself surprisingly isolated. The river to his left, an embankment thick with brush to his right, a narrow path between. He stepped over roots and rocks muttering at the ridiculous idea any seniors would risk tripping and falling in order to see the sculpture. *This is stupid. I should bring it back to the lodge. It's of me fishing. At least I'll enjoy it.*

Lifting a low hanging branch, he dipped his

head and walked through to a clearing.

"What." He said the word out loud letting his head fall back, looking at the blue Colorado sky. He clasped his hands on his head, staring at the sculpture of him and his brother fishing. His pose in the midst of reeling in a fish, where Jett held a net, his prize fish already secured.

Jim inhaled the scent of pine and mulch and faced the water, examining the rocks forming a bridge across a shallow part of the river. In a familiar gesture, he glanced at his watch hearing his teen voice encouraging a younger Jett as they took turns timing each other racing across and back.

"Go, go, go! That's the way, Jett! Twenty-three seconds!"

"You still beat me by a lot."

"I have longer legs. You'll catch up soon."

In the distance, he heard Kai start the engine again and walked back toward the hill.

I wanted to stay where we left off. Running the rocks. I bet you've never understood why I had to leave.

"How'd it go?" Kai asked when he returned.

"The path is overgrown. My memory of the sculpture was way off. I thought it was only of me fishing. Not me and Jett."

"Ouch. Don't tell anyone else that."

He blew out a breath. "I knew coming home would be hard, but this shit… I'd rather skip the past jumping out from behind every corner."

"Good luck. The truth is, Jim, you're going to have to scour and rinse your heart or you won't ever enjoy what's right in front of you." Kai waited as he buckled his seat belt. "None of you Mannis boys are good at that."

"Boys?" Jim grumbled.

"Yes. I'm including Dad too."

"You could be right, but you can cut me some slack. Tomorrow morning, I'm meeting Jett at the lodge now that we have a construction crew signed on. Do you want to be there?"

"I can't. I have to work. I trust you. I'm glad you're finding a way to give Jett a chance."

"It's important to Dad."

"Sometimes I try to remember how young he was when Mom died. We've tried with him, you know. Over the years. Leo and me."

"The reality is, things won't change until he stops drinking."

"I know. I'm just as guilty as anyone for babying him."

Her eyes steady on the road, he studied his sister's profile. Kai's dark hair came from the Mannis side of the family, definitely not their mother's side. Deep tan skin like their father from years in the sunshine. Smart. Independent. Strong. "All the Mannis *men* you put up with are lucky to have you around. Leo too."

Kai snorted. "Tell that to my husband when all the kids are screaming for attention."

"You're a good person, Kai. A great daughter. A good sister. A fantastic mother. You run a clinic for God's sake."

She turned, making eye contact for a second. "What is this?" Her laugh, suspicious. "Are you buttering me up for something?"

He grinned. "No. I'm just saying stuff I should have been here to say a long time ago."

She reached sideways and patted his upper arm. "I like this new you."

"What do you mean?"

Kai lifted a shoulder, then made the turn up the driveway to her house. "With Sofia. She balances out your natural intensity."

Jim let his head fall back on the headrest with a thud as Kai snickered. "Ah, here we go."

"Okay, okay. I'll stop for now." She took off her seatbelt and opened the door. "But Saturday…I plan to charm Mrs. Russo. You watch. I can be very persuasive."

"Kai," Jim warned with a groan. "Why are you so hell bent on match-making?"

He got out of the truck and walked around to the driver's side to look down at his sister. "You're a busy-body and you're stupid short." He took a step backward when she landed a mild punch to his arm. "Ow!"

"Oh, please." Kai rolled her eyes. "I'm your older sister and I know best. And I love you – you big dork."

Jim opened his arms for a hug. "I love you too."

Chapter 18

SOFIA OPENED THE DOOR NEXT to the entrance to the Queen Bee Bookstore and gestured for her mother to go first.

"That looks like a cute store." Her mother said as Sofia followed up the stairs to Dr. Wheeler's office.

"I still haven't been in there. We could go in after my appointment if you want."

"Let's do that and then get some lunch. Sound good?"

"Perfect." Sofia smiled to herself at the morning being off to a much better start than yesterday's disastrous ride back from the airport. In the small waiting area, she sat next her mom on the couch and pulled out her phone, sending Jim a quick text.

Sofia: At doctor appointment. All good. Mom slept well. Have a good morning at the lodge with Jett.

Her phone buzzed quietly notifying her of a reply.

Jim: Good to hear. So far, Jett's a no-show.
Sofia: Hang in there. He'll show…I hope.
Jim: For his sake, he better.

Dr. Wheeler's office door opened and Sofia stood. "We can head back," she said, smiling at her mom.

"Was there another patient here?" her mother asked.

"Probably. There's a separate door at the other end of the hall where you can depart from if you want."

"Really?"

"This is a small town, Mom. Everyone knows everyone. It doesn't ensure total anonymity."

"But at least you don't have to look your neighbor square in the eye," Cindy joked, standing in the doorway of her office before gesturing them inside. "Mrs. Russo, it's a pleasure to meet you. I'm Cindy Wheeler"

"It's nice to meet you too. Please call me Mia. Dr. Platt in New York says glowing things about you and your practice."

"That's nice to hear. Sit wherever you are comfortable. Sofia, I know you want a water. Mia, would you like one too?"

Sofia smiled at the ease and friendliness Cindy exuded. She took a deep breath and sat next to her mother's chair, removing her shoes and tucking her feet underneath her.

"How was your flight?" Cindy asked.

Mia set her purse beside her chair on the floor. "It was fine. Long. I don't travel often. I'd forgotten how tiring it can be."

"There's also the time change."

Mia laughed softly in response. "I slept like a rock last night. I'm excited today to see more of the town with Sofia."

Cindy placed two water bottles on the coffee table and sat down. "I spent my very early years here, then my family moved to Utah. But here's always where I've felt most at home." She opened her notebook on her lap. "Sofia and I have met a handful of times in the last few weeks. I'm very sorry for your family's loss. She's told me so many wonderful things about Anthony."

"Thank you," Mia said.

After several minutes of chit-chat, Cindy paused. "I usually ask Sofia where she'd like to begin. Maybe, where we left off from last time or if there are new things on your mind? Perhaps there is something the two of you wish to discuss?"

Sofia's eyes met her mother's deer-in-the headlight expression.

"We didn't really come up with a plan, did we?" Mia answered first, her voice a nervous twitter. "For me, I want to be here to support Sofia. Her father and I want her to move forward. Frank, that's Sofia's father, always says we need to 'get back to the business of living'. I think that's what we all need to be doing. After losing Anthony."

"Thanks, Mom." Sofia put her hand on her mother's. "My father has said those words my whole life. Kind of a 'pull-yourself-up-by-your-bootstraps' idea.

Cindy nodded, then jotted something in the

notebook. "What's that look like for you, Mia?"

When her mother let go her hand, Sofia rested hers in her lap again.

"Me?" Mia's voice rose an octave.

"Yes."

"For myself?"

Her mother put her hands to her chest and then gestured in her direction. "Or what's that look like for my daughter?"

The shrug Cindy gave was misleadingly nonchalant if Sofia's racing pulse had anything to say about it.

"Whatever is comfortable." Cindy glanced back and forth between them.

"So…" Sofia took over as her mother pushed back in her seat, appearing startled as if she'd been called on by the teacher in a classroom. "I think what those words mean is to get back to your responsibilities. In my case, New York. My job. I need to find a place to live since I couldn't afford to keep my apartment when I left." She set her feet back on the floor and busied herself as she spoke, moving her empty shoes from in front of her chair to the side of her chair.

"I suppose I can start sitting with Valerie at Anthony's football games again too. That sounds fun." Sofia both trying and failing to keep disappointment out of her tone.

"Valerie was…?" Cindy asked.

"Anthony's girlfriend." Mia sat up straight, folding her arms across her chest. "In fact, his fiancée. They just never got the chance."

"That must be very painful for you."

"It is." Mia chin lifted. "So many hopes."

Sofia made eye contact with Cindy. "My parents are going to start a scholarship at the school where Anthony was a football coach."

"What a wonderful and generous offer," Cindy encouraged. "Sofia and I have talked about a tangible way for her to honor her brother's memory too."

"Right." Sofia nodded. "I brought that up in the car yesterday, remember Mom? I could put together something with all the photos I've taken over the years of Anthony and his teams." Sofia smiled with enthusiasm. "Maybe others would make donations and his scholarship would be even bigger?"

"I don't know if that's what your father has in mind. Other people involved. I mean. It's *his* idea. For Anthony." Her mother directed a smile toward Cindy. "For our son."

"And, *my* brother." Sofia voice shook. "You don't want me to participate? Is that it? Because I've brought it up twice now and both times you've acted like I'm infringing."

Her mother re-crossed her legs and shot a strained grimace in Dr. Wheeler's direction before turning to Sofia. "Of course, that's *not* what I'm saying. I'm...just feeling uncomfortable talking about family business in front of a...someone I've just met."

"She's a psychiatrist." Sofia felt heat flush her cheeks as she stood. "You know what? Let's not talk. Let's go downstairs and go to the bookstore and lunch and out to the lodge and pretend this never happened." A sudden stitch in her side developed as if she'd run a city block. Sofia put her hand on her ribs and turned away from her mother to face Cindy. "Besides, I've made the decision to stay in Ashnee Valley and help Jim with the lodge and honoring his late mother's artwork. It'll be a good way for me to reboot my photography career and thank the Mannis family for all they're doing for me." Sofia clapped her hands. "How's that for getting back to the business of living?"

"Let's slow down. It's okay to pause for a moment," Cindy said.

"Sit, Sofia. Please," her mother pleaded.

Sofia remained standing. "I shouldn't have shouted. I don't know what you want, Mom. I don't know why this isn't going better. I'm sorry."

"I'm sorry too, honey."

At the shaky tone as her mother continued speaking, Sofia sat again and listened.

"I'm struggling." Mia said. "I don't have a role anymore. I don't have anything to *do*. Your father has this scholarship and you've always been so independent. Anthony needed me. Not just because he was sick. I thought my next stage was going to be as a grandmother."

"Mom." Sofia picked up the tissue box from the table and held it out. "You have your job. Your brothers and sisters and friends. Who says you won't be a grandmother? I'm sorry I haven't been there these last several weeks. I think about Anthony every day. I miss him so much."

"I know you do." Her mother blew her nose

and took a deep breath. "Okay, that's enough of that." She announced abruptly.

"If only it were that easy. Loss and grief and trying to find purpose again is difficult work," Dr. Wheeler said. "It's also okay to take time to figure it out. The two of you might try these next few days talking less as mother and daughter. Loosen those roles so you can support each other. You're brave women finding new paths."

"I like that idea." Mia nodded. "I'm afraid I've worn myself out and it's only eleven-thirty. That may be all I have in me today."

Sofia slapped her hand to her knee. "Let's go to the bookstore and lunch. I'm hungry. You're welcome to join us, Cindy."

"That's sweet, thank you. But I have another appointment coming up." She closed her notebook. "Come on, I'll walk you out."

"Thank you, Dr. Wheeler," Mia said.

"You're welcome. I'm so glad I had a chance to spend time with you during your visit."

"Mom, I'll meet you in the bookstore in a second, okay?" She closed the door as her mom descended the steps to the street below.

"Shall I schedule you for next week?"

"Yes, please, unless you have another slot open right now."

Cindy laughed. "Do you still have my cell number in case of emergency?"

"I do."

"Good. Call me if you need anything. Seriously. This isn't easy."

Jim led the way to the upstairs of the lodge, talking with Chris, the contractor and a few others from the construction company he'd hired. "My suggestion is we start from the top and work our way down. Note anything and everything that needs repair."

"I usually start outside and work my way inside, then bottom to top. But, sure. We can start this way instead."

Jim turned mid-way on the steps. "If you're telling me that's the right way to do this, then that's how we need to do it." He waved the men back. "Let's head outside and start over." The heavy clomp of work boots covered the angry oath Jim muttered as he followed the group.

Where the hell are you, Jett?

Gathered outside, he gestured for Chris to take the lead. "Listen, my brother is the one who knows construction better than me. He was supposed to here." Jim rubbed his eyes as he spoke. "Whatever, that's not important. I hired you. You're the expert. Don't gloss over anything. Tell me everything that's an issue, no matter how big or small."

"You got it. I'm going to have the guys fan off to take a look around on their own too." Chris pulled a notebook from his back pocket and gestured for the others to disperse. "Let's you and I start at the back and work our way around." They walked side-by-side through the overgrown grass around the perimeter of the lodge. "Jett's your younger brother?"

"Yep." Jim answered with a curt nod. "You know him?"

Chris tilted his head from one side to the other. "Not really. I've met him. He has a good reputation as far as construction knowledge, but I don't think I've ever worked directly with him on a job."

"You'd remember." Jim scoffed. "He's fucking unreliable."

Chris grunted. "I can't say I haven't heard that too."

"I imagine."

He quit walking when Chris stopped to look him in the eye. "I don't want to get off on the wrong foot, but I do have a question."

"Ask it," Jim said. "You don't need to mince words."

"You're the boss ultimately. Saying that, I lead my own guys and I don't put up with unnecessary bullshit on the job. I'm not in a position where I have to take this job, if you understand my meaning. How much is your brother going to be involved and how much do I need to worry about it?"

I really want to pound the shit out of you, Jett.

Jim shifted his stance, so he could look toward Mercy Mountain and took his time before responding.

I can't believe I'm going to say this.

"This lodge is my late mother's legacy. This property is going to help support my nieces and nephews going to college. It's going to be my livelihood, my sister's and my brother's. Jett is family. So, somehow, he's going to be a part of things." Jim shrugged. "Even though I'd really like to punch his fucking face in right now."

Chris laughed with a nod.

"If that makes you want to opt out," Jim continued, "I get it and I wouldn't hold it against you. But if you want the job, then know I'm not going to be cutting any corners. I want this property to put Ashnee Valley on the map."

A smile and gesture from Chris got them walking again. "I'm in. Or at least until you get my quote."

Jim pulled his vibrating phone from his pocket. "You don't need to worry about Jett. I'll look after my brother."

"Works for me."

"Excuse me a second. You go ahead, I'll catch up." Jim stepped away looking at the incoming text.

Sofia: Did Jett show? I'm pretty sure I'm looking at his truck parked downtown.

Jim: No word. No show. Where downtown?

Sofia: By Dr. Wheeler's office. Mom and I were at the bookstore after my appointment. Do you think he's a patient of hers?

Jim: No way. He's probably at the bar around the corner.

Sofia: I hope not. Is it going okay otherwise?

Jim: Yes. How about your appointment?

Sofia: Emotional. Grandmother dreams. I'll tell you about it later.

Jim: Are you still bringing your mom out

here?

Sofia: I don't think so, she's worn out. We're going to have lunch, then I'll take her back to the B&B. I could meet you at the lodge.

Jim: Can't. I have to be in Four Bears with Rafe by 2:30 to look at stone for the fireplace.

Sofia: Bummer. I'm still going to go and take more photos this afternoon.

Jim: I miss you today.

Sofia: I miss you too.

Jim: See you tomorrow at the ranch.

Sofia: Can't wait.

Chapter 19

Sofia sat cross-legged on the bed writing in a notebook as her mother listed the ingredients they would need to buy to make paella.

"I found a bakery where we can buy churros for dessert. It's not far from here. We could stop there first and then go to the grocery and then the farmer's market," Mia said.

"When did you find a place with churros?"

"Yesterday, after you dropped me off. I napped a little and took a short walk downtown."

Sofia gathered her hair into a ponytail and smiled. "You seem like you feel better today?"

"Yes. I think it was the jet-lag making me feel so out of sorts. My headache is gone, thank goodness." Mia rubbed her hands together. "I'm looking forward to meeting everyone. You know how I love cooking for a crowd."

Sofia stood and walked toward the bathroom as she spoke. "I do. It should be fun today. Kai's kids are adorable, and I can't wait until you meet Ben."

"Who else will be there?"

Sofia leaned on the doorframe of the bathroom facing her mother and counted off on her fingers. "Ben, Jim, Kai, and Leo, and their five kids. Rafe, he's Jim's friend. Dr. Wheeler was invited, but I'm not sure if she's coming. And maybe Jett, he's Jim's and Kai's younger brother. So, that's fifteen if you add the two of us."

Mia lifted her shoulders in an excited shrug. "Go shower and let's get moving."

An hour and a half later, Sofia put the last of the grocery bags in the trunk and got in the car. "Okay, next stop is the farmer's market." She glanced at the sweet little smile on her mother's face and paused before starting the engine. "What's that look for?"

"I've missed you. It can't have been easy to come here on your own. I don't know if I could have done the same."

Sofia pulled her chin back. "Sure you could have, Mom. If anyone has been strong, it's you. And Dad."

Mia nodded. "Thank you. I miss our family's old life. I miss feeling normal. I don't know if that will ever return."

"I miss the way things used to be too."

"I know you do. I'm sorry." Her mother shook her head. "Today is a good day. We take the days as they come, yes?"

"Right." Sofia turned the key in the ignition. "We take the days as they come."

And what a glorious blue-sky day it is.

Forty-five minutes later, Sofia drove under the Mannis Ranch arch toward the house at the end of the lane. The driveway was empty, including Ben's truck.

"Oh good. It looks like we'll be able to get started cooking before everyone arrives. Ben is probably at the senior center. He spends a lot of his time there on the weekends." Sofia got out of the car, opened the trunk ,and handed her mother a bag before picking up another. "I'll show you the house and the room where I've been staying. The view of Mercy Mountain out the back of the house is amazing." Sofia opened the door and walked into the kitchen first. "Let's set everything on the table for now."

"This kitchen is darling. It reminds me of the house I grew up in. Your grandmother had a refrigerator just like this, but in robin-egg blue. That's a vintage oven, if I've ever seen one too."

"We may have to improvise a bit on cooking pans and utensils. Ben's been a bachelor for a long time. He pretty much has one of everything."

Mia laughed. "We'll make do. As long as we can find a couple big pans and a big spoon."

For the next hour, Sofia washed vegetables, made a salad, and acted as prep-cook to her head chef mother. Glancing out the window over the sink, she saw the first of the family arrive as Kai and Leo's mini-van pulled into the driveway. Turning off the faucet, she wiped her hands on a dish towel.

"Kai's here."

Mia set the timer on the stove for the rice to cook. "Perfect timing for a short break."

"Hello," Leo called as he opened the door and ushered the kids into the kitchen with Kai following.

"Hi, everyone." Sofia put her arms wide. "Come in."

"It smells fantastic in here." Kai set a large relish tray on the kitchen table. "Hi, Mrs. Russo. I'm Kai, Jim's sister. This is my husband, Leo."

"Hello, everyone." Mia took off the apron tied around her waist to greet each family member as if she walked a reception line as Kai introduced her family.

"This is Will, the oldest. Then Jocelyn. And this is her best friend, Nicki.

"These are the twins Aiden and Luke."

Sofia's mother squatted to meet them eye-to-eye. "Hello boys."

Kai ran a hand along her youngest daughter's hair. "And this is Suze, our youngest."

"What a pretty pink dress you're wearing, Suze." Mia smiled and stood. "What a lovely family. It's so wonderful to meet all of you. I wish my husband, Frank, were here. He adores children. Sofia has probably told you we have a very large family."

"She may have mentioned that." Ben chuckled from the doorway surprising the group on his arrival.

"Ben, you're here!" Sofia bounced on the balls of her feet. "This is my mother, Mia Russo."

"Mia. Welcome." Ben embraced her mother who initiated the hug, her arms wide.

"Thank you so much for what you've done for our family. You and Jim especially. What all of you have done."

"Don't mention it. It's been our pleasure."

"Grandpa, Grandpa, Grandpa. Can we go out back?"

"It's okay with me if it's okay with your mom and dad. Don't mess up the picnic tables in the yard."

"Come on gang. Let's quit clogging up the kitchen." Kid voices trailed behind Leo and Ben as they headed through the house and out the sliding door to the backyard.

"I want to go in the barn."

"Can we go fishing later?"

"When do we eat?"

Kai turned to Sofia and her mom. "Leo has the patience of a saint. How can I be of help? Put me to work."

"The salad you brought looks so yummy," Sofia said.

"Do you want to prepare the shrimp?"

"Sure!" Kai answered Mia's suggestion. "I'm excited you're here. Have you ever been to Colorado?"

Mia resumed her post at the stove. "I've never been west of the Mississippi."

"What do you think so far? Did Sofia show you the view of the mountains? Dad has the best view in Ashnee Valley – other than the lodge."

"It's lovely. Very different than New York City."

"I've only been to New York once. I went to visit Jim there when he first got out of the Army. It was exciting." Kai tilted her head. "I'm more of a nature girl, I guess. I think Sofia's catching on too. She's even been fishing. She hasn't ridden a horse, so we haven't broken her all the way in yet."

Sofia rolled her eyes. "Jim wanted to take me horseback riding on day two or something. I think Ben talked him out of it."

"Speak of the devil." Kai crossed the room to open the backdoor for Jim to enter.

"Hi ladies. How's the cooking going?"

Sofia took a few steps his direction and stopped short. "Hi, Jim."

Okay, don't jump into his arms.

"Things are coming along," Mia answered in a cheerful tone and turned back toward the stove.

"Hey." Jim leaned in, stealing a quick kiss only his sister witnessed.

"Careful, you might catch flies that way." He walked past Kai as she snapped her gaping mouth closed. At the swinging door between the kitchen and living room, he turned back. "See you."

Sofia felt the skin on her neck heat at the triumphant smirk on Jim's face.

Holy shit. That was hot.

"Is the chicken ready, Sofia?"

"What?"

"Are you okay, honey? Your skin is blotchy."

"I could get you some water," Kai offered.

"I'm good." Sofia gave a wave and turned to the counter, picked up the bowl of diced chicken and brought it to her mom. She leaned behind her mother's back sending a cross-eyed look to Kai who pressed her lips together in silent laughter.

It was after the meal, when Sofia and Jim were cleaning up the kitchen, when Jett's black pickup pulled into the driveway.

"Crap," Jim grumbled.

Sofia took the pan he was holding so she could dry it as they stood at the sink together. "He was invited."

"Then why wasn't he here on time for the meal?"

"I don't know. Did he ever tell you why he didn't show up at the lodge yesterday?"

"Just that he had a situation and he'd explain later."

Out the window, Jett walked toward the house. "He looks all right. Let's give him a chance, okay?"

"What fucking choice do we have?" Jim opened the door. "Hey, bro, mighty big of you to *grace* us with your presence."

"This must be Jett."

Sofia turned at the sound of her mother's voice as she came through the swinging door.

"You look so much like Jim."

Sofia held her breath.

"I didn't know your sister was coming to visit, Sofia. I thought it was going to be your mom."

"That's very charming." Mia laughed. "And

silly. Of course, I'm Sofia's mother."

Sofia flinched when Jim shut the door with a bang.

"I'm Jim's younger brother. It's a pleasure to meet you. I apologize for my late arrival. An emergency came up and I couldn't get away until now."

"There are plenty of leftovers."

"Well, only if it's not too much trouble."

"It's no trouble at all." Mia put her hand on Jett's arm. "You remind me of my son. Tall and lean. I bet you have a hollow leg when it comes to eating."

"It's a rare treat to have a home cooked meal, that's for sure."

"Oh look, Rafe is leaving, would you excuse us for a moment?" Sofia grabbed Jim's hand and opened the back door, pulling him along. "We need to say goodbye."

Outside, she walked down the steps ahead of Jim.

"What'd you do that for? Rafe's not leaving."

"You looked like you were going to strangle Jett. Now, go get your friend and tell him he has to go home."

"I'm not making Rafe leave as a cover for my asshole brother."

"Shush!" Sofia giggled.

"This must be your *sister*. Seriously?" Jim pointed over his shoulder. "Does your mom really find that bullshit charming?"

"Maybe. Come on, let's leave Mom to fuss over your brother. It's harmless."

It was late in the evening when the shouts and hollers coming from the front of the house caught Sofia's attention. "Excuse me a sec. I'm going to check if the basketball game the guys are playing is still civil." She stood, leaving the circle of lawn chairs where Ben, Kai, Leo, and her mother were sitting as the kids ran through the yard playing tag.

The night fell dark, the croak of frogs coming from the nearby pond as she walked around the house.

"Hey, is the game over?" she asked, running into Jett walking toward her. Before he could answer, she put her hand up, quieting him at the sound of an argument.

"You need to tell her what happened," Rafe shouted.

"She won't understand. I shouldn't have ever told you. It's my business."

"Give her a chance."

"It would be better if she never came here," Jim responded angrily.

"Come on, man. Don't be like that."

Sofia walked quickly up the stairs to the house, picked up her jacket from the hook near the door and headed back outside.

"Where are you going?" Jett said from the bottom of the steps.

"For a walk."

"Alone, in the dark?"

"Yes."

She set off at a fast clip, moving down the driveway and out onto the dirt road. The light from the house and the barn would only get her so far before she'd have to rely on moonlight. With Jett following, she picked up the pace, making it a good distance toward the main road.

Something small and dark ran in front of her and she stopped.

Don't try to scare me, animal!

She marched forward three steps before noticing another small movement near the side of the road.

"I am fed up with all these stupid creatures running around out here!"

Jett jogged to catch up with her. She glanced at him, tears stinging her eyes, and hung her head.

"Come on now." He took her into his arms. "What happened back there is not what you think." He gave her a squeeze and stepped back, putting his hands on her shoulders. "There's something between Rafe and Jim, and I guess they mean to have it out tonight."

"It would be better off if she never came here," Sofia repeated Jim's words.

"That can't be about you. And if it is, he doesn't mean it. He's mad about something."

"That part I got."

"Don't write a whole story in your head, okay?"

She took a deep breath, trying to absorb his gentle scolding.

"Anybody can tell Jim's crazy about you. Hell, he'd be a fool not to be." Jett took both her hands. "Hey, when did you get the cast off?"

"A few days ago."

Jett gently massaged her wrist then placed her hand in the crook of his arm in a gentlemanly gesture. "Let's walk. I was coming around the house earlier to see you anyway."

"When did you become so gallant?"

"I'm trying." He laughed. "It's time to grow up and lose my demons."

She could see his white teeth as he grinned at her under the darkening sky.

"I'm having trouble giving up the familiar. Yukon Jack and I go way back."

"Maybe you just haven't found the thing you want more than drinking, something good that waits for you on the other side."

"You're right. But actually, I think it has found me."

"Like religion?" She glanced at the expression on his face and smirked.

"No. Like a son."

Sofia pulled him to a stop and faced him. "You have a son?"

"Apparently I do. He's four and his mother dumped him at my house a couple days ago and took off. His name is RJ."

She hugged him spontaneously and stood back. "Jett. Oh my God."

"I know. I'm going to have a paternity test done—it will take a while, but the kid, well, hell, he looks just like me."

"Who else have you told?"

"Doc Cindy. She's been helping me. She's babysitting him tonight."

I was right.

"I wanted to tell you first."

"Me?" Sofia couldn't have been more shocked. "Why me?"

Jett linked their arms, turned them around on the road and began walking again. The light from the barn came into view again.

He's leading me back.

"Why did you let me take you fishing?" He glanced sideways at her. "I thought so. You did it for me. And that day, for the first time in a long time, I was with a friend. You gave me that."

When they reached the driveway, Jett took her hand.

"You're the person who can best understand I need to reinvent myself. Sort of like what you're doing. Aren't you giving yourself a second chance now?"

Sofia smiled. "Is RJ why you didn't show up at the lodge yesterday? You need to tell Jim."

"I will. When the time is right. Soon."

"Thank you for coming after me and for telling me about your son."

"My pleasure, baby girl."

"You know it's not helping your relationship with Jim to call me baby girl. It drives him nuts."

"Does it?"

"Come on, you know it does," Sofia scolded. "Why do you do that?"

"I like you." He swung her hand playfully.

"Jett, that's not…we're not…I mean, you are very handsome, but…"

"You done?" Jett stared at her. "I like you as a

friend. I just told you that. It's a new thing for me." He grinned at her frown. "You can't have it both ways. Besides, if I wanted you, I'd have you." He lifted her arm and spun her as if they were dancing.

"Stop it." She pushed him, laughing.

"How old are you?" His abrupt change of topic caught her off guard.

"Twenty-nine, why?"

"That's what I thought, you're younger than me. The way I figure it, when you join this family then I'm no longer the youngest. I'm thirty, so you'll be my little sister, baby girl."

What do you mean "join the family"?

"Aw, shoot. I didn't mean it like that. Sofia, I'm sorry." He put his hand on her arm and squeezed. "No one could ever replace your brother. I guess I want nothing more than to have someone like you look up to me like an older brother, that's all. You have something, a grace, it pulls me up with you."

It had to be one of the nicest things anyone ever said to her.

"I bet you never saw yourself fishing with a guy like me, did you?"

"I didn't see any of this coming." Her response came out part sob, part laugh.

"Exactly. That gives me hope for my future."

"Did you ever think you'd be a father?"

Her gaze followed his across the darkness to where only the faint rise of the pasture remained visible by moonlight.

"I've dreamed of it. Even hoped for it, someday.

But I always thought Jim would get there first and show me how it's done."

"Not this time. You get to lead the way." She hugged him once more, letting out a yelp when he lifted her feet off the ground and swung her.

"I'm known for my bear hugs, baby girl."

"Stop, you're squishing me!" She laughed and squirmed until he set her down. Hearing footsteps she turned toward the driveway as Jim steamrolled toward her and Jett.

Chapter 20

"WHAT THE HELL? EVERY TIME I turn my back, you're pawing at her. 'Baby girl' this and 'baby girl' that," Jim said.

Rafe caught up standing next to him. "Dude, relax. It seems innocent."

"Shut up, Rafe. We're talking about Jett touching Sofia."

"She gave me a hug as a thank you. I talked her into giving you morons another chance." Jett looked around. "Hey, where'd she go?"

"Damn." Jim turned to face the house when the back door slammed.

"She overheard part of your argument in the barn, after I left," Jett said. "I'm walking up the path and here she comes, right when Rafe says you should give her a chance, and you, big brother, spout off that it would be better if *she* never came here. It was priceless. You're lucky she didn't take the truck and head to the airport."

"Then what happened?" Rafe asked.

"She took off down the road and I followed. I

told her not to write a whole story in her head." Jett turned away, heading toward his truck.

"Thanks, man," Rafe said.

"You're the one who *should* be thanking me, brother," Jett called over his shoulder. "You better make your move with that woman before it's too late."

"Is that a threat?" Jim smiled when Jett stopped in his tracks. He didn't like the cocky sound to his brother's voice. It was high time they got down to it.

"I'm saying, do right by her."

"Do right by her? What the hell is he talking about?" Jim directed his question at Rafe.

"You did invite her to stay longer." Rafe put his hands up in surrender at Jim's glare.

Stalking back, Jett stood two feet in front of him. "She's trying to gather up courage to get on with the rest of her life. Has the thought ever crossed your thick brain that she may be in love with you?"

"She may think she is."

Could she be?

"You're a stupid son of a bitch."

Jim stepped a foot closer to Jett. "All I see is you trying any way you can to get near her. Maybe she feels sorry for you."

"Yeah, you're right." Jett laughed with anything but humor. "You know the difference between you and her? She sees something in me, and you don't."

"I'm supposed to feel responsible for you growing up to be a drunk, is that it?"

"Un-fucking-believable." Jett swiped his hat off and smashed it back on his head. "You'll never let me be anything more, will you?"

"It's pretty convenient how you're always nearby to comfort her."

"That's enough!" Ben appeared out of nowhere and stepped between his sons preventing whomever might close the gap first with a fist. "Jett. Go. Home. Now."

"I'm not the bad guy! She was crying."

"Stop." Sofia put a hand up. "Please. There's something important that Jett wants to tell…"

"Nah, Sofia. Really. I'm not worth it." Jett walked away and climbed into his truck. The engine roared to life and he backed up in a wide turn, his tires kicking up dust and gravel when he drove away.

It was Sunday and early, so Jim hit the ignore button when his phone vibrated. He lifted the covers over himself again and snuggled close to Sofia, her leg thrown over his, her breath soft on his neck.

I must be dreaming because she's not here. Hell, I'm going for it anyway.

"You are beautiful, Sofia," he imagined himself saying when she opened deep brown eyes. His good morning kiss grew. She mimicked his groan when he lifted, draping her over his body so she lay directly on top of him.

His phone vibrated a second time and he reached to put it on silent mode.

Kai. She can wait.

He drifted back into the dream. Running his hands down the middle of Sofia's back, he cupped her bottom as she peppered kisses on his chest.

At the sudden and rapid knocking at his back door minutes later, Jim got up, wrapping a blanket around his waist.

Damn it.

Rafe held the door open and Leo followed his sister into the living room.

"Jim," Kai said.

"It's five in the morning. What's going on? Is it Dad? One of the kids?"

"It's Jett," Kai sobbed.

"What happened?"

"He was in a car accident overnight," Leo said. "He flipped his truck several times. He's in critical condition. About two-thirty this morning, he was air lifted to Rapid General."

Kai walked his way and wrapped her arms around him. "I tried to call."

"When did you hear?" Jim answered, looking over Kai, his hand on her back.

"Your father got a call about an hour ago," Leo said. "They had trouble figuring out who to contact, plus Jett's been in surgery for the last several hours."

His sister leaned back looking up at him with watery eyes. "We have to pick up Dad, we have to go."

Jim smoothed his hand along her hair. "It's going to be okay, Kai. You go. I'll get ready and meet you all at the hospital." He walked Kai and

Leo to the door closing it softly behind them.

"I'm sorry," Rafe said.

"Son of a bitch." Jim went to the desk in the living room, opening the top drawer and pulling out a set of keys. "Here are keys to everything. The house, ranch, Kai's house. Can you check on things at the ranch? Maybe look in on Kai's kids later?"

"Of course," Rafe said. "Go get ready so you can get on the road. Anything you want me to do about Sofia and her mom?"

"After last night's fiasco, I don't know if she'll even speak with me." Jim grabbed the back of his neck. "All of this is my fault."

"Don't do that to yourself."

"I'll call when I have news and we'll figure it out from there."

"What if he doesn't make it?" Sofia said to her mother, pacing the cozy breakfast nook at the B&B.

"Honey, don't get too ahead of yourself. When did Rafe say he'd hear from Jim?"

"We should have heard from him by now." Sofia's phone in her purse vibrated. She furiously scrambled through her bag and answered.

"Jim?"

"Hi, Sofia. I'm glad you're taking my calls after last night."

"Of course, I am. I'm so sorry. What's happening, how's Jett?"

"He's out of surgery and in recovery. He broke

near every bone in his body. He's got a collapsed lung, so they're keeping a close eye on that."

"Oh, no. Will he be okay?"

"The doctors are hopeful. He'll have a long recovery, months, a year, who knows. Lots of physical therapy. Guess this is one way to detox from alcohol, although I wouldn't recommend it." She recognized his shock in the situation at his out-of-place laugh.

"There's more we need to talk about," he continued.

Signaling that she needed a minute, Sofia stood and walked away from the table for a moment to speak with Jim privately. "I want to talk more too. Are you coming back tonight?"

"Not today. I'm going to stay at the hotel near the hospital. So is Kai. Leo is bringing Dad back to the ranch later today." Jim cleared his throat. "Sofia, last night…"

"Let's not do this on the phone."

"I never wanted to hurt you, sweetheart."

Her eyes teared at the crack in Jim's voice. "I know. We can talk soon. Rafe is coming in about thirty minutes. Mom wants to visit Kai's kids so Will isn't on his own with the whole crew today."

"Thank her for me."

Sofia clicked off her phone and sat down with her mom to relay the news. A vision of Jett's truck rolling into one of the magnificent Colorado fields made Sofia drop her head forward, her eyes stinging with tears. Her father had been the one to cry with her at Anthony's funeral. Silent and strong, her mother gently smoothed her hand the length of Anthony's coffin, a final gesture in taking care of her beloved son.

"Would you be okay without me for the day, Mom?"

"Do you want me to go to the hospital with you to visit Jett?"

Sofia shook her head. "I'll have Rafe take me."

"Eat something," her mother encouraged. "I'll be fine.

Sofia took a small bite of the blueberry muffin, drifting backward in time two nights ago. Jim's teasing kisses. His tongue sweeping hers. The wry smile when he tasted pie on her lips.

Will, Kai and Leo's oldest son's, face showed sheer gratitude when they arrived to drop off her mother for the day to visit with the kids.

"I need your help," she said as Rafe backed down the driveway.

"Sure. I have to stop at the ranch and do a few chores Jim asked, then I'm free for whatever you need."

"How long will that take you?"

"Maybe an hour."

"Can we stop at Jett's house on the way? I need to talk to Cindy."

Rafe stopped the car at the bottom of the driveway. "Doc Cindy?"

"Yes, I'm ninety-nine percent sure I can find her there."

"So that's why she wasn't at the ranch for dinner last night. Are they sleeping together?"

Sofia dipped her head at Rafe. "You're not serious with that question, are you?"

"No. God. Sorry. My brain's for shit today. Why would she be at Jett's house? What are you talking about?"

"Rafe." Sofia put her hand on his arm. "Last night at the ranch…"

"You don't know what the conversation with Jim was about," Rafe interrupted.

"Then tell me," she said, taking advantage of him mistaking where the conversation was heading.

Rafe backed out of the driveway on a frustrated sigh. "I can't."

Her question was one a best friend would never answer. "That was unfair of me."

He glanced her direction and grimaced. "Just trust me. You two need to talk."

Sofia nodded. "Can you take me to the hospital today? I'd like to visit Jett. Maybe Jim and I can talk more."

"I still don't get the Doc Cindy connection."

Sofia sighed. "When Jett followed me last night, he told me he just found out he has a son. I think he wanted to tell the whole family too. I'm not sure. But then he and Jim argued and, well, we know the rest. All I know is Jett says he's been seeing Dr. Wheeler, as a patient, and I guess she was helping him otherwise. She was babysitting last night."

"Fuck." Rafe muttered under his breath and accelerated. "How old is the kid?"

"Four. His name is RJ. I tried calling Dr.

Wheeler's cell phone earlier this morning. She didn't answer. I don't even know if she's aware of the accident."

"In this small town? She knows."

Fifteen minutes later, after knocking on the door and looking in windows at Jett's place, they returned to the truck.

"Let's think a minute," Rafe said.

"We should go to the hospital."

"I'll call Will. Since your mom is with the kids, he can go do the couple chores at Ben's. My guess is Cindy's en route or already at the hospital."

An hour and a half later, Sofia made her way quickly to the fifth-floor ICU after checking in at the information desk.

"Sofia!" Kai said, letting go of the hand of a little boy who sat on the waiting room chair next to her. "What are you doing here?"

"I couldn't stay away—*we* couldn't stay away," Sofia said breathlessly, gesturing to Rafe who followed.

Kai smiled at the little boy pulling on the bottom of her shirt, rubbing her hand over his head. "These are your daddy's friends, Sofia and Rafe."

Rafe squatted. "Hi, buddy."

She glanced up when Jim came out of the room across the hall and stopped short.

"Hi, Sofia."

Feeling suddenly like an outsider, she stuttered, "Rafe and I felt like we should come. I want to see Jett. We couldn't find Cindy. Or RJ."

"You knew?" Kai looked to Jim. Sofia silently blessed Rafe who made the awkward moment easier by acting absorbed in getting to know RJ. He settled into a seat and grabbed a children's book off the table.

"Let's find somewhere to talk." Jim led her down the hall to one of the private waiting rooms. Once inside, he sat on a couch and motioned for her to sit next to him, putting his arm around her. She pressed a fist to her chest at the exhaustion and worry on his face.

"Jim, I didn't know about RJ until last night. I think Jett wanted to tell everyone."

"Before I acted like a jealous ass."

"What happened?"

"He took a curve too fast and rolled his truck."

"He was intoxicated." Sofia's voice held resignation. "Where's RJ's mother now?"

"She split. I only know the story from Doc Cindy. Jett told her the mother was a drug addict and couldn't take care of the boy any longer." Jim shook his head.

"What's going to happen now? With RJ?"

"Kai is going to take him home with her tonight. He can stay with her and Leo for a few days, and then I've said I'll take him until Jett can get back on his feet." Jim squeezed his arm around her shoulder and leaned his head against the wall with his eyes shut.

"It could be several months before Jett is recovered enough to take care of RJ. What about the lodge?"

He opened his eyes and smiled. "I know. He's

my brother's son. He needs his family. I'm his family."

"But—"

Jim put his head against the wall again, watching her. "I know I asked you to stay to help. But the reality is, things are going to be on hold for a while."

Sofia looked down at her hands. "I understand."

Jim placed his hands on his knees and stood. "Let's go see him."

Outside Jett's hospital room, Ben now sat with RJ on his lap. He bounced the boy on his knee and sang a nursery song about wheels on the bus. The boy laughed and giggled adorably, and Sofia stopped in the hallway. This family that accepted her so lovingly weeks ago now poured attention on Jett's son.

"It's so sweet," she said.

"Sofia's going to go in," Jim told the group, and everyone nodded.

She smiled awkwardly, as if a spotlight was on her and everyone grasped something she didn't.

"It's a shock at first," Leo put his hand on Kai's knee to steady her as she spoke. "It will help him to know you're here."

The lights were dimmed, but even so it was immediately apparent how much equipment surrounded Jett. His body lay bandaged from the neck down.

"Oh, Jett." Sofia put her hand over her heart and stood alongside the bed. Machines hummed, breathed, and blinked. An IV drip hung from a metal frame.

Jett's eyes were closed and she took his hand, relieved to find it warm. She studied every feature of his face, from his incredibly long eyelashes to his nose with the slightest bump, she guessed from being broken sometime in the past.

"You're the only man I know who can break every bone in his body and still be vain enough not to get a scratch on his handsome face." She smiled at her own teasing. "You promised to teach me to tie flies." She let go of Jett's hand and picked at her cuticles. She couldn't remember the last time she cared about her fingernails. "Look what I've become." She held up her hands as if Jett could see.

Straightening her back, Sofia moved a chair close and clasped her hands in her lap like a schoolmarm addressing an unruly student. "Please listen." She examined each piece of equipment surrounding the bed. "When are you going to let go of a path that no longer works?" She lifted her chin. "Your life is meant for so much more." Her voice wobbled. "You're smart. And fun. And you taught me how to fish. You're going to teach your son to fish. This accident is either going to be the worst thing that ever happens to you or the best. Maybe it will pull your head out of your ass and make you face your demons. If it gets you past whatever pain pushes you to drink yourself to death, then there is no doubt it will have been worth it."

She shook the bedrail and let go, fists clenched.

"You're so lucky you have a brother. Your family loves you, and so do I. You're so damn lucky and you're acting too stupid to know it."

"Sofia?" Cindy entered the room and came to stand by her side. "Are you okay? We could hear you," she said gently. "You were yelling at him."

"I'm so sorry." She made eye contact with Jim who stood just inside the door. "I shouldn't be here any longer. I can't do this again."

Chapter 21

SOFIA LISTENED TO BEN WHISTLING in the kitchen. Glancing at the clock, she realized she and her mother would be on a plane heading home in only six hours. Yesterday's trip back to the Ben's house was somber, leaving Jim behind at the hospital seemed a practice run for her departure today. She'd vowed not to look back as they drove away, but she did. He placed his hat on his head, tucked his hands in his pockets, and dropped his head forward.

After donning her robe, Sofia padded to the kitchen and joined Ben at the table.

"Coffee?"

She nodded. "When will Jim be back?"

"Late afternoon. This is our last morning together."

Sofia took a sip of coffee to wash down the lump in her throat.

"How about you tell me one more story about Anthony?"

It seemed easier this morning to talk about her

brother than to think of leaving Ashnee Valley for good. "My stories about Anthony have all led up to the day he died."

Ben nodded.

"Anthony was in the hospital. He'd been in and out of there for the last few weeks, and he was aware he would die soon. I went every day after work." She stared at the liquid in her mug. "There was snow on the ground. Anthony loved winter. He used to play hockey, snowboard, ski, anything. So it didn't really surprise me when he asked me to help him get bundled up so he could go outside. But this was something the hospital would not permit because he was so weak. He begged me. 'What does it matter?' he'd argued." Sofia pressed her lips together. "So we snuck out."

"Troublemakers." Ben smiled gently. "What happened when you went outside?"

"He hit me with a snowball."

Ben raised his eyebrows. "I bet you didn't see that coming."

"No, I didn't. He threw another one and egged me on, but I wouldn't throw back. How could I hit my dying brother with a snowball? It didn't make sense, what he was doing. Anthony handed me a snowball at one point, and I remember staring at it like it was a foreign object. 'Goddamn it, Sofia, hit back!' He got very mad, his face all red and he was out of breath. 'Hit back. Hit back.' I wanted him to shut up." Sofia cleared her throat. "I wanted him to shut up and I told him to. Shut. Up. Get it over with."

Ben nodded. "I understand the feeling."

Her breath came in shallow gulps now. "I threw that snowball as hard as I could and it hit him right in the face." She ducked her head, a hot tear landing on her nightgown as Ben waited patiently for her to go on.

"Anthony laughed so hard he fell to his knees, and I ran over to him like a big ninny. I don't know what I was thinking. I know better." She sniffed and smiled at Ben. "I was afraid I'd hurt him because he'd fallen. It didn't even register he was laughing." She wiped her nose on the back of her sleeve and then reached for the napkin Ben slid across the table. "Anthony pulled me down on top of him and shoved snow down my back." Hot tears streamed down her face.

"He wanted to play."

"Yes." Her voice trembled in reaction to Ben's encouragement. "His doctor. He scolded me. He said it was a big mistake for me to take him outside. He said I let him get too cold." Sofia hung her head and sobbed.

"Do you think it was a mistake?" Ben asked when she'd worn herself out.

"Yes." She nodded. "I just wanted him to be my brother one more time. I'm so sorry for what I did."

Ben put his hand on her cheek. "Oh, Sofia. You were showing him you loved him."

"I was the last one to see him alive. He died before my parents arrived in the morning. I'm so selfish."

Ben took her hand. "I don't think you were selfish at all."

"I took that last chance away from them." Sofia wiped her eyes with the napkin and blew her nose. "I won't take anything else from them."

"It sounds like you and Jim…talked about children?"

Sofia nodded. "I understand. He's going to have his hands full taking care of RJ."

"I see," Ben said with a grim expression. "That's what he told you?"

"It's for the best. It's time for me to go home now." Sofia paused. "Jett's going to be okay."

"With time, yes."

"In the meantime, you have another grandson."

"Indeed." Ben chuckled.

Her words came out barely a whisper as she fought back tears again. "I'm going to miss our talks."

Ben sat back in his chair, a squeeze to her hand before he let go. "I'm going to miss you. You're like a second daughter to me."

"I made something for you. Can I show you?"

"Is it a pie?" Ben joked.

Sofia met his grin with one of her own, appreciating his humor more than he would ever know. "I'm afraid not. It's a mock-up for a book about the lodge and Catherine."

"Yes. Show me."

She left the room to retrieve her laptop and returned to the kitchen table. "I would never pursue this if you don't like the idea, so don't hesitate to tell me." Sitting close, Sofia pulled up a graphic file and slid her computer in front of Ben. "The idea started first from listening to Jim and how he wants to restore the main lodge. The grand room, for example, would be called Catherine Hall."

Ben pulled a handkerchief from his back pocket, wiping his eyes. "No one has told me about that yet."

Sofia continued. "And remember Jett's idea is to add little homes or cabins to the property. Here's the map we looked at before. He wants to name each one after Kai's children so everyone is included. I filled it in with examples."

Ben chuckled. "Suze Q House. Look there, you put the twins' houses together connected by a deck in between. That's clever."

Encouraged by Ben's response, she closed the map and opened the file for the book. "This would be an art book. Big." She gestured size with her hands. "With mostly photographs of Catherine's sculptures and also her notes and sketches from her art journals. Using the book, the photographs and notes could also be made into signs around the property to accompany Catherine's actual sculptures and incorporated outdoors on paths between buildings."

Ben put his arm around her shoulder and hugged her to his side. "Where they were always meant to be."

Sofia put her head on Ben's shoulder and kept clicking through so he could view the whole concept. "Where they were always means to be," she repeated.

"I'm overwhelmed." Ben pressed the bandana to both eyes. "You put all the ideas together? You took all these photographs?" He scrolled back to one of the handwritten notes. "I haven't seen Catherine's handwriting in years. I never read her diary."

"So, you like it?"

"Every bit of it. But how will this happen if you aren't here to guide it?"

"Your sons will do it. I don't know anything about construction or renovation. I think working on it together, once Jett recovers, will bring them closer. The way you wanted. With your blessing, I'll move ahead on the book."

"Your eyes dance when you tell me about all this. I'd be honored if you went ahead."

Her mouth lifted into a smile. A streak of sunshine in the midst of her broken heart. "It gives me purpose now that I'm going back to New York and takes pressure off other expectations."

Ben observed her contemplatively. "We tend to put ourselves and each other in boxes."

Sofia sighed, pulling the laptop in front of herself again and shutting down her computer.

"Sofia, I've spent most of my life doing what was expected of me. The only time I didn't was when Catherine died. I wasn't a good father."

"You're such a good father and grandfather."

He scooted his chair back, stood, and walked to the counter to pour another cup of coffee. "I am now. I wasn't for a time. It's easy to blame that on grief. People, even my kids, understand it to a certain degree. And it was grief, but not entirely."

"What else was it?"

"I never wanted to disappoint those who died.

Whether my parents when they passed or Catherine's memory, so I just barreled down the road I was already on." Ben sat down again. "I didn't embrace the detour or the people who were still alive. By doing that, my kids didn't learn how to do this very well either. We're still trying to bring ourselves back together. All I'm saying is talk with your family."

Sofia nodded. "I'll try."

Chapter 22

IT HAD BEEN FORTY-EIGHT HOURS since Sofia departed Colorado, and he was miserable as fuck while he waited for the elevator to open to the fifth floor at the hospital.

"Hi, Jim. Your brother is having a tough day. He's stable, but pretty much unconscious between the pain killers and the hard work his body is doing to repair itself. He'll have to stay in the ICU longer. I know this is frustrating. He is improving. That's the good news."

Jim sighed. "Thank you, doctor. Can I see him?"

"Of course, take your time." The doctor motioned for Jim to enter the room before he headed toward the nurses' station, turning back halfway there. "It can help if you talk to Jett. He may not be able to communicate right now, but he can likely hear you, and there are proven results shown from patients being encouraged."

The lights on one of the machines blinked as he surveyed the various bandages holding Jett together. What each particular machine did to help keep his brother alive, he wasn't sure.

If you don't live, I'm going to kick your ass.

He didn't say the words out loud, figuring that wasn't the kind of pep talk the doctor had in mind. Running his hand through his hair, he sat down next to the bed.

"Sofia left recently. I've been thinking a lot about Mom lately. Kai and I were lucky. We got a lot more years with her than you did. You were just a boy. She loved us something fierce, didn't she?" Jett's face remained still and peaceful. "Between your drinking and my letting Sofia go, she'd think us both fools. I know one thing—you need to quit drinking so you can take care of your boy. Jesus, Jett, you have a son."

His voice sounded awkward to him, self-conscious. Several nurses circulated throughout the ICU.

"As for me, I don't know what the hell I'm doing." Jim groaned, resting his head on the edge of the bedrail. Warmth from a hand on his head comforted and for a split second he imagined it to be his mother, the gentleness like hers. Jett's hand slowly slipped back to the mattress as he lifted his head. Standing, he leaned close, listening as Jett struggled to speak.

"You're a chickenshit."

"I should have told her I loved her."

"Chickenshit."

He clasped his brother's hand and sat down, laughing so hard one of the nurses stopped to ask if everything was okay.

"My brother called me chickenshit."

"I take it this is a good thing?" the nurse said, her smile gentle.

He wiped tears with the back of his hand. "It's the best thing."

It was late when Jim returned home.

"Hey, Rafe."

"Hey. How's Jett doing?"

"He opened his eyes and said a few words today."

"Good. What'd he say?"

"I told him I let Sofia go back to New York without telling her I love her. He told me I was a chickenshit."

"Nailed it," Rafe agreed with a bark of laughter.

"I have to fix it. I need to get on an airplane and fix it. I need to bring her back here. I love her."

"So you're asking me for permission or something?"

"No, shit. I don't know."

"You scared?"

"Fuck, yes."

"Well, that's good. You should be. This is big, man. When's the last time you felt this scared?"

"Besides every moment since I met her?"

"That's what I figured." Rafe talked over his shoulder as he headed toward the kitchen. "What you got is something at stake." He opened the fridge, handing Jim a beer. "It's about damn time too. Good or bad, that has to put some fire in your belly. Go to New York."

"Yeah?"

"Hell, yeah."

Jim took a sip of beer. "What about RJ?"

Rafe faced him with a gleam in his eye. "I'll take care of him. Me and Doc Cindy. He knows her already and I can help out. I'd like to."

"Uh huh, I bet you would." Jim chuckled following Rafe back to the living room. "There is one other thing."

"Lay it on me." Rafe sat on the couch.

"Dad fired me." Jim settled into the armchair next to the couch. "From the lodge."

Rafe sat forward. "No shit? Ben?"

"That's the one." Jim put his feet up on the coffee table. "I guess fired is the wrong word. Demoted. I'm not in charge anymore. He wants someone with a bigger vision," he said, adding air quotes.

Rafe nodded. "Like your girl. Or Jett for that matter."

Jim pulled his feet from the table, landing his boots on the floor with a thud. "Screw you. Thanks for the support."

Rafe waved his hand up and down. "Sit down. Come on. You know what your dad's doing."

"What?"

His friend rolled his eyes. "Your dad thinks the sun rises and falls with you. You're the only person who thinks the lodge is a requirement or a test you have to pass before you're forgiven by your family for being gone all these years. Remember how we'd talk about guys who were their own ghost sniper in the Army. They took themselves out, missed the victory, because they didn't understand the mission. You're the assist, dude."

Jim sat again, putting his head back and closed his eyes.

"Who really needs to have a challenge like the lodge when he gets back on his feet?"

"Jett."

"Who decides what kind of life she wants, kids or no kids? Or, for that matter, if she wants you."

Jim groaned. "Sofia."

"Hell, you decided everything for her by not telling her the truth. Ease up. You don't have to be everyone's protector in order for them to love you." Rafe sat back with a look of satisfaction on his face. "Now go pack for New York so I can play house with Doc Cindy for a couple days."

New York

No matter how many military flights he'd been on heading overseas, anticipating violence at the other side, nothing could compare to the agony of this middle-of-the-night return to New York. His boyhood pain hadn't gone away in a flash of lightning, but in his homecoming he'd realized his family still needed him, and he them. Sofia's presence eased his way.

I don't want to save her. I don't want her to save me. I don't want a desperate love between us out of fear of losing someone again. What I want is the chance to show up for her every day of the rest of my life.

Several hours later, he landed in New York. Turning his phone back on immediately, he listened to her voice, asking about his family and ending the message with an almost whispered, "I miss Colorado."

He put his sunglasses on as he walked through the airport, not giving a rat's ass about the need to hide his eyes.

If you let me, I'll never miss another chance to tell you I love you.

First, he came to talk to Mia and Frank Russo—not for old-fashioned reasons or because Sofia wasn't the one to make her own decisions. Partly it was because of her brother, Anthony. Funny to put so much stock in a person he'd never met, whom he would never meet. He wanted something…the blessing of yesterday before asking her to take his hand and walk forward…together.

Repositioning his hat, he took a deep breath and examined the skyline retreating as the ferry headed toward Staten Island. He'd left in such haste he wasn't sure her parents would even be home and had no plan for how to get to the Russos' house.

At the station he ended up hitching a ride with a guy he asked for directions. The kid had played football for her brother a year ago. Waving as the young man drove away, Jim turned to face the front door and found Mia Russo smiling at him.

"What brings you back to New York?"

"Mia, stop it." Frank reached around his wife and extended his hand. "Jim, it's good to see you. Come on in. Sofia's not here, she's in the city."

Stepping inside, he stood still. Moving boxes were piled everywhere. People milled in and out of rooms, eating and talking. Kids ran and laughed, weaving around corners.

"I should have called first. My apologies."

"Don't mind the mess or the people. This is all family." Mia waved as a way of introduction, and several people smiled and said hello. "We're getting ready to go to the homecoming game later. Anthony's scholarship is going to be announced at half-time."

"You want a drink, son?" Frank asked.

"Yes, sir," Jim said.

"I thought so. You look as miserable as Sofia does. Let's go sit in the den."

"I'm coming too." Mia followed. "How's your brother doing?"

After he gave an update on Jett's progress, the three of them sat on leather furniture, facing each other. Jim sat on the smallest love seat he'd ever seen. His eyes traveled the trophies and football photographs adorning the walls.

"We're retiring and downsizing. This room will be hard to pack. We'll probably save this one for last," Frank said.

"Maybe we should get it over with." Mia looked to Frank who nodded his agreement before she continued. "You know Sofia took every one of these photographs. Did she tell you we're moving?"

"No. I'm glad I came, then. I wanted to see the place where Sofia grew up, the place where Sofia and Anthony grew up together." He took a swallow of his drink and let his eyes rest on his glass. "I'm more nervous than I thought I'd be." He laughed, looking up.

Mia put down her drink and squeezed in next to Jim on the tiny couch. "Tell us why you're here."

"For God's sake, Mia, if the man wasn't terrified before, he is now."

"Mr. and Mrs. Russo, I love your daughter." Facing Sofia's mother first, then her father, he paused before continuing. "I shouldn't have let her leave Colorado without telling her."

He could do awkward silence with the best of them, but the impatient sigh from Frank Russo was a particular kind of torture.

Sofia's mother shifted close, linking her arm with his. "Why didn't you?"

"I've been thinking a lot about legacy. I left home as soon as I could after my mother died. I'm not sure she'd be proud of how long it took me to go back."

"Mothers are always proud." Mia squeezed his arm. "Go on."

"I thought I could make up for lost time by fixing up Mercy Mountain Lodge for my dad. Truth is, my brother, once he's better, will be more suited to leading that effort. It's been tough fitting back in with the family and living up to expectations."

Frank nodded. "We've been having some conversations here too about expectations. With Sofia."

Jim set down his drink and took a deep breath.

It's now or never.

"I didn't tell your daughter how I feel about her because I can't necessarily give her all the things she wants." Jim clasped his hands together. "Or that the two of you want." He looked from one to the other. "I have a ...a medical condition. I can't have children. Of my own. I've known for most of my life."

"I'm sorry to hear that, son."

He closed his eyes for a brief moment trying to hide loss when Sofia's mother lifted from the seat next to him. He opened his eyes when she said his name.

Mia held out her hand for Frank to hold. "Anthony, had he lived, would probably have had as many children as your sister Kai. And we would have loved them dearly. More than we can ever put into words."

Jim nodded.

"We can't speak for Sofia," Frank added. "We can only tell you that we're a family struggling our way through our grief. I'd say you and your family can well understand this type of pain."

"Yes, sir."

"Jim," Mia said. "None of us are going to come out the other side of loss, if we don't expand our ideas about how and where love is available to us."

"Thank you, Mrs. Russo."

The pocket door to the den cracked open and a small boy dressed in an oversized football jersey stuck his head in.

"Great-Aunt Nora wants to know if the cow-boy is going to take Sofia back to Colorado with him because she said if Sofia won't go, she'll go." At that, the boy's face turned bright red and he slid the door shut. A huge round of laughter came from outside the room.

"Well, I guess I can't lose, then."

Mia and Frank appeared desperate to maintain straight faces before bursting with laughter.

He didn't stay much longer, going on a quick tour of the house with Sofia's mother before he walked the gauntlet of slaps on the back on his way to the front door. He declined riding with the majority of Sofia's relatives to the high school, accepting a ride from Sofia's Uncle Rudy instead.

"Are you sure you don't want to sit with the family before half-time?"

"I'd rather not take any attention away from the ceremony for Anthony. I'll make my way over after," Jim answered, his nerves kicking into high gear as he was dropped off.

"Understood. Good luck."

Chapter 23

"How are you doing?" Delia asked as they walked arm in arm through the parking lot of their old high school toward the stadium.

Sofia shrugged. "I'm okay. It feels weird to be back here."

"At the school? Or do you mean, New York?"

"Both."

"I'm sorry it all came to such an abrupt ending in Colorado. Have you spoken with Jim since you returned?"

Sofia shook her head. "No. I left him a voicemail earlier today. Kai sent me an email. It's only been a few days, but Jett is doing better already. Awake more."

"That's great news." Her best friend patted her arm. "I'm so glad tonight is a mini-heat wave so we won't freeze in the stands during the game. I'm so proud of you."

Sofia stopped walking. "Why?"

"Because you've been through a lot and your

family has too. Anthony would love the scholarship."

"He would. God, I miss him so much."

"Me too. Besides my dad, he was probably the only other man I felt safe enough to be my real self around," Delia said.

"Anthony loved you, you know." Sofia giggled. "Remember when he made you laugh so hard that chocolate milk came out your nose?"

"You do recall he called me *squirt* from then on, right?"

"It feels good to laugh," Sofia said. "I'm glad I'm staying with you tonight. I don't think I could go back to the house. Everything is in disarray with my parents packing to move. Thanks for being here for me."

Her best friend put an arm around her shoulder and squeezed. "Always."

Sofia would have liked the team to play better, but the Port Vincent Tigers were down by fourteen points at the half. Nervous butterflies skittered through her as the band finished and the football team came back and gathered mid-field for the ceremony to honor Anthony. Making her way down the bleachers with her parents, all her aunts, uncles, and cousins, she couldn't help but smile as her big, boisterous family took their place next to the team.

"Thank you for joining us for this special halftime presentation to honor our late colleague, Coach Russo," the principal said. "If you would, please stand for a moment of silence."

Sofia shook her head and breathed in deeply as the crowd rose, removing their hats, and the stadium went quiet.

Anthony.

"Now, I would like to welcome Coach Anthony's father, Frank, to share a special announcement the Russo family wishes to share with all of you."

She steeled her emotions as her dad walked to the microphone and cleared his throat.

"It would mean the world to Anthony to see all of you here tonight to honor him. It means the world to us, to me. To his mother, Mia; sister, Sofia; and our entire family. Thank you."

Lifting her chin, she barely kept tears from tipping over the edge to her cheeks as the crowd applauded.

"Anthony was very proud of his time at Port Vincent as a coach. So proud of his boys. His coaching staff. He would have stayed here forever. I really believe that. This place. This school. This city. This was *his* dream."

She made eye contact with her dad at the emphasis to his words and smiled back.

"Now and in the future we can remain part of that dream through two scholarships the Russo family is offering to the high school."

Turning to her mother, Sofia held up two fingers as a question.

"One scholarship is for outstanding performance in high school athletics," Frank said. "This will be in Anthony's name. The second is for outstanding talent in the arts. This will be in our daughter's name, Sofia. She's an outstanding photographer."

She covered her face with her hands and wept as her mother's arms encircled her.

"Please, indulge me for one more moment." Her father paused as the crowd's encouragement grew in volume and enthusiasm. "Grief is all the love stored up that you don't know where to put when someone is gone. It's so easy to store it. To shy away, in our pain, from sharing that love ever again. We must not grow scared to dream for ourselves again. Let us be brave, each of us, going forward."

Sofia lifted her gaze, her heart pounding at the handsome dark-haired man looking at her from the sidelines as the first shouts of "Coach Russo" floated into the air.

He waited until the Russo family was seated again before climbing the steps toward Sofia. He took off his hat with a smile to her friend Delia who scooted down the row to make room for him as he approached.

"Is this seat taken?" He sat, laughing with relief when Sofia climbed onto his lap in a full body hug.

"You're here."

"I was hoping we could talk after the game."

A tear fell as she nodded enthusiastically and hugged him again.

"Don't cry, sweetheart." Over her shoulder he took in the expectant look from Sofia's relatives.

"That's it?" Sofia's Uncle Rudy asked. "After the game?"

Sofia sat back. "That's my uncle. He's teasing."

"Frank, I think he missed your speech a few minutes ago about bravery," Rudy added, scanning the rest of the family, many of whom nodded in response. "Boy, you didn't come to the house this afternoon without a purpose."

"You were at my house?" Sofia asked.

"Earlier this afternoon. I wanted to see where you and Anthony grew up and to speak with your folks."

"Ignore my brother," Mia Russo said. "He's—"

"Right." Jim finished her sentence then leaned his forehead against Sofia's. "If I do this in front of everyone, will you come back with me to Ashnee Valley so we can do this again? Just you and me."

"This is so romantic," Aunt Nora said.

"What'd he say? What'd he say?"

"He's going to declare himself to her for all of us to see," Aunt Nora explained to the group. "And then he's going to do it again in Colorado when it is just the two of them."

"He's not going to propose?"

"Rudy," Frank scolded. "Go ahead Jim, we're ready."

"Dad!" Sofia put her hands on his cheeks. "I'm sorry about this."

"Okay, everybody." Jim laughed and lifted Sofia from his lap and knelt on the steps next to her seat. "Sofia, I came here tonight because I want to give you everything you want in life. I didn't give you the chance to decide any of that for yourself because I was scared to tell you how I felt before you left. I don't want to spend another day apart from you. There are some things we'll need talk about between us. I'd like to do that part alone."

He grinned when Sofia pointed at her family and zipped her lips in warning.

"Will you come back to Ashnee Valley with me on the red-eye tonight?"

"Yes."

He stood, leaning forward to hand tickets to Frank, Mia, and Delia. "These are for you to join us soon. I'd like you to spend some time with my family as part of any decisions the two of us may make."

Then he put out his hand, pulled the woman he loved to her feet, and kissed her with all that he was and all he hoped to be.

For her.

For him.

For love.

Jim tucked his jacket underneath the seat in front of him and fastened his seat belt. "Ready?" he asked, glancing at Sofia next to him.

"Ready." She pulled her hair into a ponytail. "Same as last time or are we changing the rules?"

"Lightning round. No passes. Sex questions permitted."

She rolled her eyes. "Right."

He cleared his throat. "When I say I want to wake up with you every day of the rest of my life, do you know it to be true?"

His heart beat fast as her eyes held his, a soft pink spreading to her cheeks.

"Yes."

"When I tell you I want to give you everything you want in life, do you believe me?"

"Yes," she answered softly.

"If I told you I can't give you everything, something you may want, do you think you could still want me?"

Her voice was gentle as she took his hand. "What's going on? You can tell me."

"I don't want to lose you, Sofia. I didn't say how I felt before you left because I can't be everything you need. I can't have children. Not biologically. I've known for most of my life. It never really mattered to me until you."

"Do you want children?" she asked, her eyes searching his. "Is that important to you?"

"No." He shook his head. "I've known it wasn't possible for so long, I've become comfortable with how things are. I just...want you. But I know that may not be enough."

He waited, suffering through the long pause before she responded.

"I want to do this differently," she said.

"I understand..." He stopped talking when she squeezed his hand.

"No, you don't." She shook her head. "This. I want this. I want a different life than my brother wanted. After he died, I felt I should make up for the fact that he was gone and do all the things he would have. I was scared I'd disappoint my family. But I don't want to miss out on being with you."

She shifted in her seat, her knees bumping his as she lifted the arm rest and wrapped her arms around his neck. "It's my turn. When I say I want to wake up with you every day of the rest of my life, do you know it to be true?"

Her hopeful face lifted to his, her big brown eyes seeking.

"Yes."

"When I tell you I want to give you everything you want in life and that I want you, and that's enough, do you believe me?"

"I do."

He put his hand to her cheek, an enormous grin on his face as she shifted closer.

"I love you, Jim."

"I love you too, sweetheart." His lips met hers, igniting a slow-burn kiss that made him groan when the steward stopped to ask Sofia to put her seatbelt on.

"Good game." Sofia laughed as she moved back to her seat.

"We have a few more hours, we can keep playing." He leaned close to her ear as the airplane taxied to the runway. "I could suggest all the ways I'd like to give you pleasure as soon as we get home."

The sexiest smirk whispered across her lips. "Yes, please."

Chapter 24

Colorado…two weeks later

"WHAT'S THIS PLACE?" SOFIA SAID, her arms around Jim's waist as he brought the horse to a stop in front of an old structure on the edge of the lodge property.

"For now, it's shelter. Look up." Dismounting, he held her around the waist and set her on the ground. Angry black storm clouds pushed in. At the top of Mercy Mountain, lightning struck.

"Where did a storm come from so fast?"

"You know Ashnee Valley by now, weather moves in quick and, fortunately, moves out nearly as fast. We'll have some shelter inside from the rain. Definitely the last burst of warmth for the season."

He estimated they had five minutes before the sky opened up.

"What about your horse?"

"There's an overhang around back. I'm going to tuck her there. You go ahead inside. I'll be right in."

As he secured Blaze, she waved his direction through missing slats in the wall at the back of the cabin.

"Did someone live here?" she asked when he entered, walking the perimeter of the room.

Not a piece of furniture remained except an old chair, a reject from an ancient dining set, he imagined. "No, it's an old hunting cabin. I brought the blanket so we could sit." Jim glanced around as rain started. "I guess we can sit as close to the front door as possible since there is no longer a room, besides the frame at the back."

"I'm not sure I've ever been in a storm while half in and half out of a house."

He smiled at her amusement, pulling the single chair across the room. He pulled items out of the satchel, placing them on the blanket.

"You should stay over at this end, Sofia, so you don't get wet."

He glanced at her, pulling out the water bottles in slow motion when she gave him a look that, unless he was crazy, was as hot as July. Unsure of what she was up to, he determined not to interrupt its potential. After toeing off her shoes, she made her way across the blanket until she stood in front of him, nudging his knees apart.

"I thought you said you were starving," he said.

She put her arms around his neck and bent forward, wiggling her behind. "I can wait."

"Are you trying to seduce me, madam?"

Removing his hat, she flung it behind her onto the blanket.

"Enough talking," she said, eliciting a satisfied groan from deep in his chest. He put his thighs together and brought her down, straddling his lap. He started slow, running his tongue over her upper lip and sucking on her bottom lip.

"Sofia." He whispered softly. She squirmed on his lap, anxious. Without breaking his kiss, he slowly unbuttoned her shirt, pushing it aside, smiling with satisfaction as he took in the pink bra with the white lace. Her chest rose and fell, her breath accelerating, her nipples hardening under his gaze.

"May I?" He unfastened the front of the bra and pushed it open. "So pretty." Jim centered his hands over her nipples, barely touching each with the center of his palms.

Sofia arched, pushing her breasts further into his hands. "Yes."

When he lifted his hand to her cheek, she turned, placing a kiss at the center of his palm. He took her arms from around his neck, pinning them behind her back. He lowered his head to suckle her breast, flitting his tongue back and forth, nipping the bud with his lips. He lifted his head. "Do you know how sexy you are?"

Grinning at her face flushed bright pink, he coaxed her to stand. "Turn around." He held her hips loosely as she turned before pulling her back down on his lap, resituating her so she straddled him again, this time her legs facing out. "This is what I was dreaming about on the horse. Lean back."

"But…" Her voice carried worry as she let her

head rest against his shoulder.

"It's okay. It's just you and me."

He brought her arm up and wrapped it around his neck as his other hand cupped one of her breasts and she arched, pushing her hips forward.

"That's it."

"Oh, God." Sofia moaned as he cupped both her breasts.

"Shhh," Jim whispered, "let me."

"Please."

"So. Damn. Polite." He timed each word with the release of the buttons on her pants, slipping his hand inside and circling her folds.

"So. Damn. Wet." His hand drifted, his fingers dipping in, then stroking up to circle before slipping back in. When she moaned, he whispered her name and opened his legs, forcing her to do the same. He gently pinched one of her nipples in rhythm with the circle of his fingers. He strained against his jeans, her bottom, for any sort of relief. The slightest scrape of his teeth on the smooth skin of her neck brought her orgasm pulsing around his touch. He savored every crack of thunder from the storm and her fluttering breath until her climax was spent. The softest "oh" escaped and her arm fell limp by her side.

After several minutes, Jim gently lifted Sofia off his lap and stood. "I'm starving."

Her eyes settled on the brick in his pants when he stood. "Um," Sofia said. "I could…"

He shook his head. "I'm going to check outside." He could have walked straight out the back of the ramshackle house, but instead his addled brain had him opening the front door and announcing Sofia should stay inside. At her muffled giggle he turned fixing his eyes on hers.

"Put your pants on, woman."

She nodded and pressed her lips together. He let his eyes slip down to her still open shirt and bra.

"Jesus." He growled and closed the door behind him.

The storm left the air unusually warm for the ride home. Sofia rested her head against Jim's shoulder, the fingers of her left hand intertwined with his as they re-crossed the Talking Fish River. It was getting dark and voices carried across the valley and small shapes were visible dancing back and forth in front of the bonfire outside the log house.

"Our home is full of family and our yard is full of Kai's children." Jim nuzzled behind her ear. "On the back of a horse is the only way to be alone with you."

"Our home. I like the sound of that."

"It feels right."

"It does."

"Are you all right with having RJ for a while? In addition to Rafe?"

"Of course."

"I'm kicking all of them out for the night, including RJ."

She turned. "Why would you do that? Where will RJ go?"

"RJ is staying at Dad's. Rafe is going wherever, that's his problem. Doc Cindy is going to drive Jett back to the rehab facility after."

"After?"

He studied her profile, tucking her hair behind her ear, running soft kisses up the side of her neck. "Sofia, I couldn't love you any more than I do. At least, I don't think I could. But everything's possible when it comes to you and me." Moving his hands beneath her shirt he ran his fingers lightly over the smooth skin along her stomach. His fingers continued upward, lightly brushing the underside of her breasts. Damn, he loved the way she arched her back, the way she always leaned into him. "I love you."

"I love you too."

Sliding his hands down her sides, he reached into his jacket pocket, pulled out a small box and held his hands in front of her, his arms naturally embracing her.

"I want to be your husband. Tonight. Everyone's back at the house waiting for us, including the sheriff. He's a justice of the peace."

"You're awfully sure of yourself," she said with a gleam in her eyes.

"I'm sure about you." He leaned in, smiling when she lifted her shoulder as he tickled behind her ear with soft kisses.

"And it just so happens my parents and best friend are at the house too. Clever man."

Her rich laugh floated over him. "Lucky man." He sat tall again, her back against his chest. "This ring belonged to my Mom." He opened the box.

"Dad gave it to me the first day I got home to Ashnee Valley."

She shifted to look at him. "With me?"

"With you." He grinned as she faced forward again and held out her hand. "You're ready for this?"

She nodded as he slipped the ring on her finger.

"Will you marry me, Sofia? I love you."

Nearby the soft glow of fireflies answered each other in the tall grass.

"Yes."

Chapter 24

SOFIA PUT HER KEY IN the lock to Mercy Mountain Lodge, turned the handle and pushed the door open.

"Surprise!" Her best friend Delia said, suddenly appearing.

Sofia slammed her hand to her chest. "What are you doing here? I thought you went back to New York with my parents yesterday. You scared me to death."

"Don't be silly. It's just me."

Sofia tried to look past her friend blocking the doorway as if she owned the place and wasn't letting anyone in. "Um..? That still doesn't explain what you're doing here."

Delia stepped onto the porch, closing the door behind her and rubbing her arms up and down. "It's cold today."

Sofia gestured to the door again. "We could go inside, where it's warmer. Then you could tell me what's going on." She turned at the sound of a vehicle, watching a black limousine head toward the lodge. "Who is that?"

"This was going to be a surprise, but you got here earlier than expected."

"Since I don't know what's going on yet, it is a surprise."

Delia laughed. "Right. Okay, don't freak out."

"Why would I freak out?" Sofia called after Delia as she went down the steps to greet whoever was in the fancy vehicle.

"It's a wedding gift."

"A limo? You know I hate that corny stuff." Sofia sighed. "So does Jim, by the way. It's cliché and besides we're already married."

"Yes, you are. But we're still having a real reception in the spring. The gift is not the limo, it's the person inside. Rodney Kendall from Boston."

"Who? I don't know anyone named Rodney. Wait. Kendall? As in Catherine Mannis? I mean Kendall. Kendall Publishing?"

Delia waived away the driver and opened the back door to the limo herself. "The one and only," she said, looking back for a brief second. "Hello, Mr. Kendall. Welcome." Delia stepped aside as an elderly man emerged from the vehicle, wearing a camel-colored winter coat and black gloves.

"Miss Kincaid. It's nice to meet you in person. I once had the pleasure of seeing you perform a few years ago when I was in New York."

"Thank you. It's nice to meet you too. This is Sofia," Delia said with a sweeping gesture to where Sofia stood frozen on the porch.

"Cat got your tongue, baby girl?"

Sofia whipped around looking at her husband

and the rest of the Mannis family crowded in the open door to the lodge.

"Shut up, Jett." Jim grumbled. "I told you not to call her that."

"She loves it." Jett grinned from his wheelchair. "Don't you, sis?"

"Rodney." Ben stepped past his sons onto the porch. "Welcome. Please come inside."

Taking her by the elbow, Jim gently led her inside first, smiling when she gasped. A string of lights hung from the rafters over a small but elegantly set round dining table in the middle of the room.

"Jim, what is going on?" Sofia whispered. "Why is he here? What is all this?"

"It's a business meeting. For you and Kendall Publishing. About the book you talked to my dad about."

"Mrs. Mannis," Rodney Kendall interrupted. "I apologize. I should first say congratulations to you and Jim on your recent wedding."

"Thank you."

"I take it you know I'm Catherine's cousin?"

"I...of course...call me Sofia...um."

Ben clapped his hands. "We'll be on our way."

"Wait," Sofia said as her family left through the front door one by one. "You're all leaving?"

"I'll pick you up in an hour." Jim winked.

"I'm afraid I have a very short amount of time to hear your pitch for the book about Catherine's sculptures." Rodney said.

"My pitch?"

"Yes, for your photography book. I realize this could appear like an easy sell. All in the family. But I assure you there is none of that involved in making my decision."

Sofia took a deep breath, shrugged off her coat, and gestured to the table set for two. "Have you ever been here before, Mr. Kendall?"

"This is my first visit to Ashnee Valley and the lodge." He held the back of her chair as she sat, then took his own seat. "When Catherine died several years ago, I was unable to come to her funeral. Unfortunately, I was in the midst of a rather messy divorce at the time. I didn't want the property here to somehow get in the mix. Legally, that never would have been the case. But the level of spite from my ex-wife could have caused unnecessary concern for Ben and the kids."

"I understand. But you're familiar with Catherine's work? You've seen her sculptures?"

"Of course."

"But not in person? Catherine's sculptures are outdoors around Ashnee Valley. People can touch them that way. She wanted that."

"I've only seen photographs, most recently yours. Ben shared them with me. Is that normal for an artist to want people to touch her work?"

"Normal?" She smiled, picking up the carafe from the middle of the table and pouring in each cup. "Normal is what is expected. Isn't that what Catherine left behind in Boston?" Sofia took a bite of the homemade carrot cake set before her.

"This is from Patsy's Diner." She motioned her fork toward the dessert. "It's delicious."

"Why do I get the feeling I am now pitching you instead of the other way around?" he asked.

"Mr. Kendall. I'm so honored that you are interested and I appreciate that you came all the way here to meet with me. And it doesn't surprise me that Ben would set up such a generous opportunity on my behalf."

"But…?"

Sofia sighed. "The truth is, I can make a photography book happen on my own if need be." She met his raised eyebrow with one of her own. "And to be honest, all in the family *is* part of any decisions I make these days."

"You remind me of Catherine. You're direct. Go on."

"I know from researching your cousin's background that she gave up her place to you as the heir to a very lucrative publishing company. And I know you built that company into a news empire." Sofia smiled. "You don't publish coffee table books."

"On that you're correct. Nonetheless, I suppose at my age I now have the luxury of indulging in projects that are simply of interest to me."

"This town is where your cousin lived and loved and raised her beautiful family. They are your family too. And now my family. I live in the house where your Aunt Marjorie spent her last years. This lodge is where your cousin sculpted. This room we're in is going to be named after her. Catherine Hall." Sofia pushed her chair back and stood. "Would you come with me. I want to show you something downstairs."

Sofia led the way to the basement, flipping on the lights at the top of the stairs as they descended. "This is Catherine's life work, besides some sculptures around Ashnee Valley. I have all her notes and sketches too. I would love to do a book together. But you and the Mannis family could do so much more. The lodge, the town, her children and grandchildren those are also a part of who she was."

Rodney examined a sculpture as he spoke. "What are you proposing?"

"An investment in Mercy Mountain Lodge. In the restoration of this special place. To install all Catherine's sculptures for generations of families to visit and enjoy. Ben likely didn't tell you he's willing to sell the ranch to see it happen."

"No, he didn't mention that part." Rodney gave her a contemplative look. "If I stayed overnight, would you be willing to show me around the property tomorrow? To tell me more about the plans for the lodge?"

"Not just me," Sofia said as they headed back upstairs, "but Jim, Jett, and Kai would do that too."

Jim stood just inside the door. "Would do what?"

"Has it been an hour already?" Sofia asked. "Show Mr. Kendall around the area tomorrow. We could even go to the sculpture garden near the river."

"Sure, that's a great idea. It's unlikely you could fly out tonight with high winds coming in anyway. Dad would enjoy having you stay at the ranch."

"Show me the way, I'll follow you two there."

"So…" Jim rubbed his hands together. "It's a yes? To the book?"

With a wry smile, Rodney's eyes met hers briefly. "It's a start."

Epilogue

Six weeks later

Sofia stretched her neck trying to see out the window from Ben's kitchen. "What's that noise?"

"Jett's medical scooter," Jim and Ben said at the same time.

"A scooter!" Delia got up from the table and joined Sofia at the window. "Oh my God, look at the two of them, that is hysterical."

"What he's doing is tearing up all the grass between the house and the barn." Jim grumbled.

"It doesn't matter," Ben said.

"He's got RJ on his lap, driving." Sofia snickered.

Delia leaned over the sink to see. "He is *so* cute."

Sofia bumped her hip to Delia's. "Which one are you talking about?"

"RJ, you goof." Delia walked back to the table and sat. "I don't think anyone would call Jett Mannis, cute. Would they Jim?"

"You're asking me? Yeah, not cute."

"Hey." Ben laughed. "Give your brother a break, he's got a lot of work to do to learn to walk right again. Time playing with his boy is just as good therapy, if you ask me."

Delia pushed back from the table. "I'm going out there. Anyone want to join me?"

Sofia waved her friend on. "Nope, have fun. We leave for the airport soon." Staying at the window, she kept watching and laughing.

Ben put down his newspaper. "What's she doing that's so funny?"

"Standing on the back of that thing, riding along. She's probably singing her butt off because both Jett and RJ are cracking up."

Walking to the window, Jim's arms settled around her waist. "It's nice that Delia could come back for another visit so soon. Your friend is not at all like you."

Sofia pouted. "What's that mean? I can be spontaneous too. I'm fun."

"Yeah, you are." Open mouth kisses skittered up her neck as Jim's fingers slid higher underneath her shirt. "And, sexy. Hot as hell."

Ben cleared his throat.

"Sorry Dad." Jim chuckled. "When did you want me to drop you off downtown?"

"When the physical therapist gets here. The session will be at least an hour Jett told me. You'll need to watch RJ since Sofia's taking her friend to the airport."

Sofia leaned against the counter sipping the last of her coffee. "What's happening downtown?"

"Dad has a date."

Ben shuffled his newspapers into a pile with a long-suffering sigh. "It's not a date."

Sofia bounced on the balls of her feet. "Ooh, who with? No wait, let me guess."

"Good luck, he's keeping it a secret."

Sofia pulled a chair out again flopped down and rested her chin on her hands, studying Ben's face. "I know who it is."

Ben's lip curled up in amusement. "I bet you do."

"What? Who?" Jim asked. "I hate this telepathy thing you two have going."

"Plain as the nose on your face." Sofia giggled.

"Easy as pie." Ben chuckled.

"Patsy from the diner!" Jim's voice rose. "It's Patsy? You have a date with Patsy? She's so much younger than you."

"No she's not, she's in her late sixties. I'm in my late seventies." Ben pushed his chair back and tossed his papers into the recycle bin next to the back door and stopped at the kitchen window. "Uh, we have a new development."

Jim joined his dad at the window. "I thought it got kind of quiet all of a sudden."

Sofia turned when footsteps pounded up the back steps and RJ burst through the door.

"I have to pee."

"Go right ahead." Ben motioned to the hallway, then moved aside when Sofia came to window.

"Holy smokes." Sofia whispered. "That's some kiss."

"Sure is," Ben said.

"Looks like Delia's sending Jett off to war or

something." Jim scooped up RJ when he ran back through the kitchen heading toward the door. "Whoa there, buddy. How about you come with me today. We can stop by Aunt Kai's house so you can play with Suze. How's that sound?"

"Okay." RJ wriggled in Jim's arms until he set him down again.

At Ben's, *coast is clear*, Sofia opened the door. "RJ, why don't you go say goodbye to Delia. She has to head home to New York today."

"She's funny. I like her."

Sofia ran her hand over RJ's hair. "I know for a fact that she likes you too. You'll see her soon. She'll be back when the weather is warm because we're having a big party at the lodge."

"I can't wait." RJ shouted as he headed outside and she closed the door.

Sofia gathered her keys, purse and sunglasses from the counter then kissed her father-in-law on the cheek. "I want a full report later about your date."

Jim slipped his arms around her and squeezed. "What about me Mrs. Mannis? Can I…do something…things…later…for you…to you…?"

"Mmm, I made a list." Sofia answered with a quick kiss.

"Good Lord, the air is thick in the valley." Ben gave a snort and left the kitchen.

"That's quite a look you have on your face," Jim teased.

"Who me?" Her voice rose in feigned surprise.

"Yes, you."

Sofia opened the door and turned back to her

husband. "It seems Delia and I have something intriguing to talk about on the drive to the airport."

Acknowledgements

For my husband and son, thank you always for your love and encouragement.

Barbara Bettis asks all the right questions to bring forth the best story possible. Thank you so much for editing *Firefly Duet*. Thank you to The Killion Group Inc. for the gorgeous cover and expertly shepherding the book to the finish line.

I can't give praise enough to Pub-Craft who manage my social media, website and marketing. Laurie Cooper is a joy to work with in every way.

The original draft of *Firefly Duet* was written many years ago and in the time since has been significantly changed. Thank you to my earliest readers who offered critiques and gently nudged the beginning of my journey from writer to published author.

To Jim and Sofia, who waited so patiently for their story to be told…thanks for sticking with me!

Books by Becca Maxton

MERCY MOUNTAIN SERIES
Dragonfly Dance
Firefly Duet

<u>Coming Next!</u>
Honeybee Rhythm

For sneak peeks and the latest release dates
visit *www.beccamaxton.com*

About the Author

Becca Maxton is a contemporary romance author. She writes sensuous (dare say, steamy) and encouraging stories about rocky road detours leading to resilience and romance. Her characters are brave women and men facing challenges together and finding love.

Becca is a member of Romance Writers of America. She lives in Colorado with her husband and son.

Follow Becca Maxton on Facebook and Instagram @BeccaMaxtonAuthor or visit www.beccamaxton.com. She enjoys meeting and connecting with readers online.

Manufactured by Amazon.ca
Acheson, AB